NO LUCKY NUMBER

SECRETS OF STONE: BOOK FIVE

ANGEL PAYNE & VICTORIA BLUE

NO LUCKY NUMBER

SECRETS OF STONE: BOOK FIVE

ANGEL PAYNE & VICTORIA BLUE

WATERHOUSE PRESS

*My dedication always starts with my
amazing other half, David. Husband,
best friend, father extraordinaire. I'm forever
grateful for your support and encouragement, even
when I don't quite believe in myself. You and our
family are my entire world. I love you.*

*Second, I must thank my amazing friends, Elisa and
Anna. I can't imagine getting through a day without
you. With this book, more than any of the others
so far, your encouragement, advice, and honest
feedback helped me believe I really had the ability to
make it happen. You are the best friends I could ever
hope to have, and I love you with all my heart.*

—Victoria

CHAPTER ONE

Forgive me, Father, for I have sinned.

Thinking about Drake Newland and Fletcher Ford at my family's Thanksgiving dinner table was doing things it absolutely shouldn't to the space between my thighs. Tingling things. Hot things. Utterly illicit, utterly inappropriate things.

They were my bosses, for heaven's sake.

Sort of.

They were...associates? Colleagues?

Friends.

All right, I could live with that. We were *friends*, that was all. No harm in having friends, right? I mean, I was friends with Taylor, Claire, and Margaux too. No one thought anything sideways about that.

So why didn't I feel better when fitting the same template over those two beautiful men? Why did my face rush with heat when I thought of Fletcher brushing against me to grab something off the printer? And why did my pulse quicken at the memory of Drake pressing against me in the hallways at Stone Global Corp, the multinational, multifaceted conglomerate where we all worked, always seeming to time those moments when the interns passed by with the mail cart, so no one would notice the contact? Why, after nearly every one of those interactions, did I have to duck into the restroom and splash cold water on my face? I couldn't even count the lunches that went uneaten because I completely lost my appetite to the butterfly maelstrom that took over the real estate in my stomach when I was around one—or worse, both—of them.

Sort of like right now. Lamb, turkey, roasted root vegetables, butternut squash, dressing, cranberry sauce, and homemade bread—all my American and Russian favorites—were a culinary joy for my eyes but slammed into a wad of nervous nausea in my stomach.

All because I'd dared to think about my two "friends."

And realized that those men belonged in my friend zone as much as penguins belonged in the desert. While my brain waddled through that bizarre territory, I totally zoned out to my Uncle Nikolai's lean-in before he gently implored, "What's wrong, Natalia?"

"Uhhh... Hmmm?" Pushing food around on my plate, I blinked across the table.

"Are you all right?" Mama pounced on the interrogation, forcing me to look down the table to where she sat, in her usual place at my father's left side. "You've barely touched your stuffing, and usually you're on your second helping by now," she charged. "Are you coming down with something, Natalia?"

"I'm fine, Mama."

"She's probably coming down with something." My mother jabbed a finger at her sister. "Serafina, check her forehead."

I scowled as my aunt, the good old-fashioned human thermometer, invaded my personal space and placed the back of her hand across my forehead.

"I'm fine." I batted lightly at her hand. "Stop, please. I just had too many snacks while we were cooking. My goodness! Seriously, you're all fussing like a bunch of hens."

Though I added a little laugh to my teasing tone, Mama

*hmph*ed and then scolded, "Perhaps you need a little more fussing and a little less working." She wasn't one to miss the opportunity to give a good dressing down, especially over *dressing*. "I am right, Talia Maria, and you know it. Work, work, work. *Always* work for you, girl. Late nights. Weekends. *Business trips*. Strange cities; different companies. Why do they send *you* and not the men?"

Katrina re-entered from the kitchen, straining her arms to carry in a platter of freshly sliced meat. "Times have changed, Mama."

"*Thank you*." I gestured my big sister's way with a swooping hand, palm up.

"Didn't say it was right." Katrina plunked the platter down and shot me an arched brow. "Just that it was different." And frowned enough over her final word to emphasize her actual intent.

"All that stress," Mama went on. "All that *danger*. It will throw your cycles off for good. Then what will happen when you *finally* think about babies?"

"Oh, dear God."

I lowered my head into one hand. Uncle Nikolai rumbled out a chuckle.

Aunt Serafina clucked and shook her head. "Well, she has a little time, Olga." It was another voice of support that wasn't, already implied by her tone—as well as the grand finale I knew was coming. "Seeing as how she's single now."

Ta da.

I lobbed a Hail-Mary pass to divert everyone, appealing to the famous Perizkova clan's sweet tooth by cheerfully shouting, "Who's ready for pie?"

"I am!" Anya piped up, eagerly pushing aside her plate—

unfinished vegetables and all—but hanging on to her fork, now propped vertically in one of her adorable fists. "Is Gavin coming today? Is he bringing the special pie with the extra chocolate and smiley face?"

Forgive me, Father—for now I have really sinned.

Because at the mere mention of his name, I was overcome with the desire to stuff my hand inside the bird and use it as a deadly weapon. I wished the man didn't exist at all—and knew, beyond the shadow of a doubt, I'd have no problem driving a drumstick through his eye and a carving knife into his gut.

The force of my reaction was so vehement, even my best efforts to veil the rage wasn't enough. I knew that before even rising to help clear the table, just as I was certain Mama would take note of every tight nuance on my face. And yes, just as I was sure she'd get in her disapproving *tsk* as fast as possible too.

"What have you done with that sensible mind of yours, Natalia?"

Clank. I winced as my frustrated tremble caused me to nearly break a couple of the Lomonosov china plates when they clattered together. She had no idea what my "sensible" mind had been through because of Gavin March. None of them did. "*Mama*—"

"And your heart. What happened to your *heart*, Natalia?"

I was cut off from responding—probably a good thing— by a high-pitched gasp from the other side of the table. We all snapped our stares over as Anya thrust her chin out, struggling to keep it from quavering. "Auntie Talia left her brain somewhere? Aaanndd her heart?" Her eyes, bigger than a Bychkova doll's, brimmed with tears.

"Anya. *Honey*." Katrina dipped her head toward her daughter. "It's just a figure of speech, like I explained to you the other day."

"B-But Luke Porter at school told me if I beat him in dodgeball again, he'd take my brain out of my head and mush a tumor on it."

"And what did I tell you to do about Luke Porter?" Katrina's prod emulated, nearly tone for tone, Mama's chastisements at me. I had to duck my head now, hiding my disgusted grimace.

Anya huffed out a growl. "That he's just a silly boy," she mumbled, "and that I should let Luke win."

Maybe I was going to shatter the china anyway. Over my sister's head. But Mama was too fast, already nodding Anya's way and then chiding, "Your mama's right, *myshka*. Boys want to be the hunters. It is in their nature to be aggressive."

"They're also just growly when they like a girl, honey."

It tumbled out faster and louder than I'd intended, prompting Papa and a bunch of the other men in the living room to stop rubbing their bellies, but I didn't feel a shade guilty about interrupting their sports talk and game wagers. I *did* feel bad that Anya's perturbation just seemed to deepen.

"But Daddy doesn't growl at Mama," she stated. "And Gavin never growled at you."

"That's exactly right," Katrina concurred.

And here it all came again.

The crappiest thing was, I couldn't even blame Anya for throwing that slippery eel of a subject into the mix. I simply had to just grin, deflect, and attempt to change the subject to something more swoon-worthy than the snow job Gavin had buried all of them beneath.

I hated this.

Hated. It.

And there in lay the real sin—the real transgression I needed forgiveness from. I could no longer stand being in the same room with my own family. I could no longer relate to the very people who raised me from infancy—who clothed and fed me, who loved and guided me into the young adult I was today.

And in turn, that made me sadder than one of the wide-eyed dolls I'd just likened to Anya. Once upon a time, I was the one who loved these family gatherings the most. My family, even with all its vibrant extensions and colorful craziness, meant the world to me. When I was a teenager, having a built-in support system and network of friends in an otherwise strange city made the transition almost seamless when we moved to San Diego. Even Katrina's pubescent fits were manageable because I could duck out and go to our cousins' house just a few blocks away.

But now, hearing that jackass's name, along with the adoring way everyone crooned and sighed and venerated it, made me want to scream. He really had snowed them all. They had no idea what Gavin was really like, when no one was around or watching him morph into a violent bully, and I had no choice but to keep it that way.

That wasn't even the worst part of things.

One night several months ago, I'd gone to Katrina's to babysit. I had a key so I'd let myself in. Huge mistake. I walked in on Katrina and her husband, Victor, mid-flow into one hell of an argument. Katrina was already sporting a bright-red handprint on her cheek, which had made me freeze in the doorway, until my sister saw me and implored me to leave.

Like the coward I was apparently raised to be, I'd done just that. Tucked tail and run—bolting on my sister and the man who was physically abusing her. I'd felt like shit about it, especially because the incident had taught me a huge lesson about my family as a whole. Even if I chose to come clean about Gavin and his abuse, they all would have just turned blind eyes and adored him at the next holiday gathering regardless. And horribly, it became a tipping point for my relationship with my sister too. Something broke inside me that night—something deep and profound. Katrina was my big sister, the one person I'd looked up to my whole life. She didn't do everything right, but she always tried, making lemonade out of even the worst lemons, and I'd grown up admiring that spirit in her. But seeing the defeat in her tear-filled eyes that night, I knew there was nothing I could revere there. Just the opposite. I couldn't be that woman.

I *wouldn't* be that woman.

My resolve had only intensified when I tried to talk to her about it a few days later. Katrina had blinked like I'd just suggested we run for the border and get matching tattoos in Tijuana, doing her best to act like she didn't know what I was talking about.

But the key term there? *Act.* I couldn't subscribe to a moment's worth of her wide-eyed wonder, even when she recited like a practiced verse to a favorite poem, "What do you mean? My husband would never hurt me. He loves me."

"I saw the mark on your face!" I'd countered. "And you— you were crying, Katrina."

"Nooo." She waved a dismissive hand, her voice sing-songy like she was pacifying a child rather than her young adult sister. "You were seeing things, silly girl. You don't know what you're saying."

At once, my voice had dropped in volume and tone. I was furious with her and the way she'd trivialized the incident. "I know what I saw, Katrina. I heard him yelling before I even got into the house that night. He was angry with you about something. Really angry."

Her voiced dipped to match mine then, and she stepped in close, almost in warning. "Well, I deserved to be yelled at. I was being foolish."

"He *hit* you! Don't you dare say you deserved that!" I didn't budge, wanting her to know I was strong. Perhaps even needing to prove it to myself. She could come to me. Confide in me. I'd be there for her. Good Lord, *someone* needed to be. "You shouldn't let him do that!"

But she'd turned away, completely readjusting her posture and demeanor. The creepy subservient wife was back. "Don't be silly, Natalia. You don't understand marriage."

And there it was.

Natalia.

Affording me no more respect than Mama.

I'd folded my arms across my chest, whether to protect myself from her act or to comfort myself from the transformation I was witnessing in my own sister, I wasn't quite sure. "Clearly I don't."

"One day you'll see. If you're lucky enough to have a man love you, to marry you and take care of you. You'll see. Now run along and don't say any of this nonsense to anyone else. Do you hear me?"

She'd transformed again to finish it off, her face hardening, her eyes flashing. And again, I'd wondered if I'd ever really known my sister at all—but had restrained my stunned gape in favor of a glare to match the burn of hers. "Yes," I bit out. "I hear you."

I just wish I hadn't.

Even now, months later, I remember going to my room and crying until I fell asleep. It had happened. Somewhere, somehow, Katrina had become one of them. One of the adults we used to talk about in our room at night. The adults from the old country we didn't want to be like, didn't understand. We'd ridiculed them for not changing when they came to America.

But then *she'd* changed. Regressed. Bowed for them. And for the man who'd given her a home and a family—and bruises.

That night, another recognition had hit. Hard. I'd changed too. Marriage was no longer part of my life's dream or my heart's desire. I didn't want any part of being married if it meant my husband had the right to hit me without consequences. Why would a man hit a woman he supposedly loved—even if he lost his temper?

Correction. Why would a *real* man do that?

As the question haunted my mind, I gaped over into the living room, where Katrina was dutifully replacing Victor's beer with a fresh frosty bottle. He never looked away from the TV to thank or acknowledge her. And Katrina herself? The robot maid from *The Jetsons* showed more life than her. She moved with stiff automation, her entire face tight—and, I suddenly realized, caked with heavy makeup. Was she hiding secrets of her own? Had Victor hit her even that morning?

My belly turned over, threatening to bring my food back up in spectacular fashion.

How had this happened?

How had this become my life?

Why was I sitting here, during a feast that should have been about celebration and family, trying to summon happy thoughts so I didn't vomit in rage all over my plate?

The road was wretched, twisted, and tormenting. And

despite my most violent efforts to keep the memories at further bay than my nausea, they surged up and into my mind anyway...a relentless invasion...

My own situation with Gavin, and how it unfolded, flooded my mind, unwanted and unbearably clear, as though it were just yesterday, rather than just over a year.

CHAPTER TWO

One year ago

The culture I was raised in was stuck in another time. My parents grew up in Russia and then immigrated to the United States, along with most of their siblings and friends. They'd only been my age, their early twenties, when they came to a country that for all its openness was still a foreign and strange place. Everyone continued to live near one another once they settled in San Diego, clinging to their traditions and old-world lifestyle to have at least a few familiar things around them. Most of the principles were beautiful and respectable, albeit antediluvian to outsiders—especially the practices of matches and marriages.

And the constant conflict that dogged my existence from the second I turned sixteen.

Typically, when a young lady became of dating age in our community, her parents began arranging suitable dates for her. Suitable, as in boys from within our society. Granted, it wasn't as rigid as some crazy religious commune, but it was easier for a girl to, say, get to the mall or the movies if "properly accompanied" by a guy the whole community already knew. Choosing to date an outsider meant rigorous scrutiny and evaluations, a trial by fire that most boys eventually caved beneath, deciding the woman just wasn't worth the hassle. In the end, the elders of the community got their way anyway, so most girls simply didn't fight all the unwritten rules from the start.

And thus, the scythes that had cleared my path to Gavin March.

We were introduced by Aunt Serafina. She knew his aunt and so on. He courted me properly and was always the perfect gentleman while doing so. He had impeccable manners around my parents and loved ones, and since our first handful of dates were huge family events, he worked hard to make a good impression on them. It worked. My parents pushed me to take the relationship to the next level, even though my instincts were already clanging with reservations. I just wasn't that into him, to put a modern phrase on the whole thing.

But despite the feelings I had—or didn't have, more appropriately—I agreed to go on a private date with him. The entire night, I'd felt like poor Anna with that asshole Hans in *Frozen*. The charmer back at the palace was handsy and physical as soon as my parents weren't anywhere around. By the end of the night, I felt like I had been in a brutal wrestling match. I didn't mind a kiss here and there, but Mr. March turned into an octopus: hands everywhere, all the time. When I got home that night, I cried into my pillow so no one in the house would hear me. Our families were already talking about an engagement party and were way more excited about our relationship than I was. It was a runaway train, and I wasn't sure how to stop it.

The next day, I pulled Claire, Margaux, and Taylor away for an emergency girls' lunch. I needed advice from my three closest friends in the world, and I needed it fast.

We met at a local Mexican restaurant, where I completely went off the rails and ordered their *grande carne asada* fries. Margaux had a sad little salad in the middle of her plate, making the mountain of food on mine look even more obscene.

"Babycakes," she stated. "You cannot eat that at lunch unless you're hitting the gym for the next three hours."

"Leave her alone." Claire came up between us, two street tacos on her plate.

"But that's like nine hundred and seventy-three carbs in the potatoes alone." Margaux peered at the plate again and then at me. "Can I have a few?"

"Margaux! Seriously!" Claire chided. "Clearly, she's crisis eating." She didn't speak again until we all sat down in a booth in the corner, scooting around until everyone was comfortable. "So, what's going on, honey?"

"Crisis eating? Is that a thing?" Taylor asked while placing her napkin across her lap.

"Apparently not for you!" Margaux volleyed while signaling toward Taylor's plate, piled high with the daily *especial*.

"Shut. Up. Do you see all of this? Watch this magic act. I'm going to make it all disappear!" Taylor was the girl every other one hated. She was naturally thin and had the appetite of a high school boy. It was nature's cruel joke on the rest of us.

"Don't rub it in, skinny girl!" Margaux crossed her arms in front of her, looking with obvious envy between Taylor's and my overloaded plates.

Taylor stuck her tongue out, and Margaux retaliated with the one-finger salute while stealing another fry from my spud mountain.

"This is ridiculous. Oh, my God. Get this away from me." She slid closer to Claire, where she would be farther out of reach of my lunch. The rest of us watched her antics, silently holding back our laughter until a giggle finally escaped from

Taylor. Crack in the proverbial damn. We all enjoyed tossing and turning along the giggle floodplain until the mirth left our systems and we were mopping up mascara tracks from the tears.

Sometimes laughter really was the best medicine.

And sometimes, a girl really needed to know she had a posse at her back—with laughter, fries, or otherwise—when it most mattered. Like now.

"Why don't you just get some?" I finally challenged Margaux, teasing her by dramatically sliding an ooey gooey fry into my mouth. "It's a legitimate question!" I countered to her scowl. "Indulging once in a while won't kill you."

"Because." She stabbed her fork into her salad. "You see the camera up in the corner there?" She used the utensil to motion toward the little black device mounted behind some towering potted palms. "And there?" And then did the same thing toward the opposite side of the room, where the black box was keeping company with some artfully arranged sombreros.

We all turned to look and then answered in unison, "Yeah?" I heard the amazed lilt in mine, because honestly, I'd never even glanced up into those crevices.

"The *hombre* who owns this place?" Margaux returned. "While he arguably has *la comida mas fina*, will not think twice about selling still shots from that security footage to the highest tabloid media bidder of yours truly stuffing her face with his *carne asada* fries. So needless to say, those are things that must be indulged in in the privacy of my own home." She finished by stuffing the salad on the end of her fork into her mouth and making a big show of how *delicioso* it was.

Taylor sighed with meaning. "Don't you get tired of it?" she asked. "I mean, are you ever just tempted to go into hiding?"

"Been there, done that! Doug Simcox, anyone?" Margaux looked around dramatically like she was polling an audience.

Claire reached behind her sister and gave her shoulder a squeeze. We all knew the memories of the DougMar days were hard on our friend. But the conversation had just taken a strangely perfect turn, giving me a great segue for why I had summoned them here with just a few hours' notice.

"So...this is kind of why I needed to talk to you all."

Margaux dropped her fork with a clatter. Anyone in the restaurant who hadn't been staring because they recognized either her or Claire was doing so now. "Has something been published again?" Her typically bronze complexion went pasty.

"No!" I waited a few beats for the attention to disperse before continuing. "No. I mean it. It's nothing like that. This... this is about me. I'm sorry." It tumbled out of me nearly in one frantic sentence. I felt terrible about causing so much anxiety with one poorly worded sentence. "I should have thought about that better. Should have worded that differently."

"Oh, shit." Margaux buried her face in her hands. "No. *I'm* sorry, Talia. I was selfish to assume it was about me." She finally looked up and grabbed my hands in hers with a grip so fierce I winced. "Please, honey, that was so egotistical."

"For Christ's sake, woman." Taylor batted at our joined hands. "We're used to it. So just get on with it, you." She motioned to me with her chin. "Sweet baby Jesus in a car seat, all this drama. Got my knickers in a bunch."

Margaux and I both turned slowly to look at our beautiful blond friend, having at us in her Southern accent, and we couldn't help laughing all over again. Taylor's way with words could break up any serious moment. Margaux reached across the table and stole another fry off my plate before motioning me to go forward with the conversation.

"It's...Gavin." I let out a heavy sigh. Just releasing his name into the universe felt like a bit of the weight lifting off my spirit.

"I don't like that guy. I'm just going to say it." Of course, Margaux didn't hold back.

"Margaux. For heaven's sake. Let her talk," Claire chastised.

Margaux gave her a twisted look. "You don't like him either. You told me that."

"Oh, my God." Claire shook her head and covered her face with her hand. "Why do we take you in public? Seriously, you need to be medicated or shock collared."

"Or something," Taylor chimed in. "Owww! Did you just kick me?"

"Absolutely not." Margaux smirked. "I had a muscle spasm." She took a long drink from her iced tea before winking at Taylor, who bent forward to rub her shin beneath the table.

"Shit. Why didn't you kick Claire? *She* said it. I was just agreeing."

"Have you met her boyfriend?" Margaux volleyed. "He'll be in my office in ten minutes after we get back, lecturing me about his fragile dust mite...blah blah blah." She waved her hand back and forth, feigning boredom.

"Fairy," Taylor and I corrected in unison.

"Riiiight. Faaairy." Margaux concluded with a dramatic gagging sound from the back of her throat.

Claire tossed out a mildly perturbed side-eye, though we all knew how stuff like that only egged Margaux on. "Talia, honey, *seriously*—do you want to meet after work without her?" She just went for it with an exaggerated finger stab at Margaux.

Margaux sat up taller. "So we *are* getting serious now? Perfect. You know I don't like that douche canoe, Talia. I've never made that secret info. But has something happened?"

I stared down at my twisting fingers. "We—uhhh—well, we went out on a date, you know, without being around family. And—well—he was...ummm..."

Claire slid a hand over my wrist. "It's all right, honey. Take it at your own pace."

But that was the problem. "At my own pace" meant I'd never speak about any of this. *Ever.* Dating, relationships, intimacy... None of this was remotely natural for me to talk about under *normal* circumstances. "He was...aggressive," I finally stammered. "And I told him I didn't want to go so fast, but he kept pushing himself on me." My words were quiet, almost inaudible by the end, especially in the din of the afternoon crowd in the restaurant.

"Did he force you to do something you didn't want to do? I will hand him his balls in a teeny tiny Dixie cup."

We all nearly spurted our drinks.

"No," I answered quickly. "I mean, I guess not. We kissed. And it was like he sprouted six hands and they were everywhere all at once. And when I said stop, he would. But then he would start again. I don't know. I'm not sure what I even want you guys to say to me about all of this. I just thought...I mean, I guess I expected it to be different, you know? That I would feel different. That it would be something I wanted to be happening while it was happening. But all I could think of was making him stop. And then thinking, what if I told him to stop and he didn't? What if he hit me the way Katrina's husband hits her?"

I gasped the second the words escaped me and quickly covered my mouth. "I shouldn't have said that," I finally rasped. "Please, *please* forget I said that."

"Okay." Claire pulled in a huge breath, along with Taylor and Margaux, before murmuring, "Let's come back to that very disturbing and *not* okay sentence in a minute. But first things first. Let's focus on you." She reached over again, taking my hands in hers this time. Her eyes, so big and brown, had never seemed so intense. "*Listen to me*, honey. If you aren't enjoying it when Gavin touches you, then don't let him touch you. It's your body, and you get to say who touches it and who doesn't."

"You understand that, right?" Taylor pressed forward too. "This isn't some weird, backwards way of the old country, is it? You're not expected to just submit to something you don't want to be doing, are you?"

I shook my head once and went on in just as small a voice, "But I think my family really likes him. They want us to be together. They're already talking with his family about an engagement."

"Holy crap," Claire uttered.

"Butter my ass and call me a biscuit," Taylor stuck in. The fact that she didn't get a laugh out of anyone was a marker of how serious the subject had become—which was, to be honest, deeply reassuring. I really wasn't crazy. Or, as I feared even more, a prude or a bitch.

"But I'm really confused," I confessed. "I don't want to live the rest of my life with someone I already don't like."

"Of course you don't," Claire replied.

Taylor, maintaining her forward tilt, pushed her plate off to the side. "Can someone explain something to me?" she demanded. "Why are your parents talking about your engagement, though you and Gavin aren't? How did it become *their* decision?"

"That part *is* tradition," I explained. "Though not every village from the old country is that way. It's just something my family hung on to. Parents believe they know what's best for their children, despite the fact that it's not a life-and-death kind of thing anymore. They still want to be sure the men their daughters marry will be good providers, husbands, and fathers to the next generation. It's weird, I know, but they consider it proof of their love."

Taylor snorted. "That doesn't make it right."

"No, it doesn't." I glanced around to all of them as I said it. "I mean, it all stems from the best intentions, but now, in modern day, it just seems controlling and intrusive."

"So physical abuse is just a bonus, then?" I didn't blame Margaux for being obviously upset. She was sensitive when it came to abusive men, and we all knew it.

Still, I felt the need to defend, "It's not like that."

"What's it like, then?" Margaux snapped back, clearly in knee-jerk reaction.

"Margaux." Claire tried to play peace maker. "*Relax.*"

"No, I'm not going to *relax.*" She mimicked her sister's tone while pushing her plate to the side for the waiter. I held on to mine because I wasn't quite ready to part with my insane caloric commitment just yet. "No man should ever lay his hands on a woman in anger. Ever."

"I agree with you, and you know that. But your indignation is putting Talia in a place she doesn't deserve and a position she certainly doesn't need to defend right now." Claire gently rubbed Margaux's back. I couldn't help but notice she was one of the few people Margaux didn't eviscerate when they touched her.

"Sorry again, honey." She smiled in my direction.

"You have every right to be upset," I soothed. "I will *not* defend the behavior, in any form." I started twisting my fingers again. "A...A few days ago, I walked in on my sister and her husband having an argument. Katrina had a bright-red handprint on her cheek, and I'm sure it was because Victor had just slapped her. I asked her about it later when we were alone, and she treated me like a child. It was like I couldn't possibly understand what it was like to be married and that his behavior was all part of being in a relationship. Honestly, I thought about so many things, right then and there. I thought that if that's what being in a relationship was all about, I never wanted to be in one."

Claire reached across the table and stilled my wringing hands. "Well, I can guarantee you, that is not what it's about. *At all.*" Her brow furrowed. "So, is this a normal thing? In your culture?"

I mirrored her frown. "Sadly, I'd say yes. I think women tell themselves to grin and bear it if the man checks all the other boxes, you know?" I released her hand to list them off on my fingers. "If he's a good provider, good husband, good father, all those things...so what if he loses his temper once in a while and they have to take a little 'handling'? The rest makes it all worth it, right?" I paused, sensing everyone needed the break as much as me. "We're almost conditioned as girls growing up to think that it's normal. I mean, when I think back on my childhood now, I definitely can remember my dad striking my mom. Right in front of us. And if we cried? He would tell us if we didn't keep quiet, we'd be next." I shook my head, trying to make the hazy memories a little clearer and wondering why I'd blocked them out for so long. "I can't believe I'm only remembering that now."

"Was it ever more than a slap here and there?" Taylor spoke up then. "My mom had a few boyfriends who smacked her around. I hated it. I used to kick and punch them when they were hitting her, just to make them stop. I usually ended up on the floor beside her."

"Not that I can remember," I answered. "I think one of my uncles may have been a little more aggressive with my aunt, though. I remember she used to have bruises on her face pretty often. She would joke with the other women that she was just clumsy. Now that I know better, I have to think the other women knew what was going on." But silently, I think about Katrina and her marks—and wonder if I would have accepted the same excuse if I'd not seen the glaring truth with my own eyes.

Margaux took a big gulp of tea and set the glass down with a thump before tilting her head and dramatically boring her stare into me until I met the ferocity of her gaze straight on. I had to hand it to her, the girl knew how to get everyone's attention. "Will you promise to tell us if that jackass ever touches you in an inappropriate way? Even slightly?" She finished by chugging the rest of her glass, likely to keep herself from saying anything more colorful about Gavin.

I nodded in silence, suddenly feeling profoundly embarrassed. I was smart—I mean *really* smart. I had a *master's* degree. I excelled at any job or task I took on. So how was I sitting here, having to make promises to my friends about an action plan in case my boyfriend decided to hit me?

I didn't know whether to laugh or cry, so I dug deeper into the pile of fries in front of me, even though my stomach wanted to reject it all.

★ ★ ★ ★

I dated Gavin about a month longer before giving in and having sex with him. He pressured me relentlessly. It was my first time, so I really didn't have a "benchmark" to compare it to, but he seemed careless, selfish, and quick. On the other hand, maybe I'd wanted too much. Had watched too many romantic movies and swooned over too many mushy love songs.

Afterwards, despite trying the "suck it up, girl" speech on myself a dozen times, I went into the bathroom and cried. I pulled out my phone, desperately trying to remember where Claire, Margaux, and Taylor said they'd be that night and wondered which one would be most readily available to meet me somewhere, but Gavin barged in because I'd forgotten to lock the door—and his obvious aversion to the word "boundaries." He found me sitting on the toilet with my panties around my ankles and my cell phone in my hand.

"What are you doing?" His ominous scowl matched his ugly tone.

"J-Just checking email." The excuse was lame, but I was never good at lying.

"While you're on the shitter?"

"Uhhh... I guess so?"

"Well, I have to piss. Are you done? Fuck it; never mind. I'll just go in the shower when I'm in there."

I almost dropped my phone. "You're going to urinate in the shower?"

He shrugged. "Doesn't everybody?"

He turned to face the shower, so I took advantage of his distraction to stand, pull up my panties, and pull down the T-shirt I had borrowed from his drawer. "I—ummm—don't think so. I mean, I don't." I fought not to sound as disgusted as I actually was.

He shrugged again, careless of the fact that he was completely naked, his spent penis flopping back and forth as he gathered his razor, soap, and towel. "Well, you're a prude. There's probably a lot of things you don't do."

Despite the shield of his shirt, which I felt like shucking and burning, I shivered and hugged myself as if I were nude again. Tears prick the backs of my eyes, but I vowed not to shed them in front of him. "G-Gavin?"

"What?"

"Why are you being so mean?" *Don't cry; don't cry; don't cry.* I swore not to be ridiculed for yet another thing tonight.

"For fuck's sake, Talia. I'm not being mean. Just telling the truth."

Then he was gone. Physically, just into the shower—but emotionally, at least a million miles away. And like the idiot I was, I just stood there and stared. Hoping for something? That he'd...what...invite me in with him? Would I have even accepted?

No. My purpose was deeper. I needed to keep seeing him like this, for my own good. To realize how deeply I regretted giving this Neanderthal my virginity. Nothing about the experience had been remotely pleasant or enjoyable. And now that I was looking at him with all the lights on, it was just as I suspected; *everything* about him was dinky and disappointing.

I was galvanized then. I dashed back into the bedroom, scooped up all my things, and let myself out as quickly as possible. I didn't want to talk to him any more that night. I wasn't sure I ever wanted to talk to him *again*. I craved a scalding shower myself, along with time to collect my thoughts and figure out what I was going to do with this disastrous relationship. Another month of my life had been spent as his lapdog—an entire thirty days I'd never get back. And now I had gone and complicated the mess even further by finally giving in and having sex with him. But that was on me now. All of it. Especially the remorse at entrusting one of my most precious belongings into the care of a clumsy asshole. I'd carry the weight of that mistake on my soul for the rest of my life.

CHAPTER THREE

When all was said and done, the total time I wasted on Gavin March was about a year. I tried ending things with him on numerous occasions, but without fail he'd come up with a reason why we couldn't break up. And yes, he thought of *everything*. One time, it was my father's health scare. Another, it was because his mother had planned an elaborate surprise birthday party for me, and a breakup would embarrass her in front of her friends and family. It was always something, and it always felt so legitimate.

A cage without a key. A nightmare without an end.

Especially when he started getting physical with me.

The first time, it was a shove against the wall. He scared me so badly that I shut down into silence for an hour, but his quick apologies and frantic kisses finally broke through my stupor. He told me how much he loved me, begged endlessly for my forgiveness. He promised that he'd just lost his temper after a bad day at work. It would "never happen again."

The cage had gotten another padlock.

For days after that, he was the sweetest he'd ever been to me. Crazy as it sounds, there were parts of me that were almost glad it had happened. A new side of him emerged, one I'd never seen before. A side that was kind and nice. A side I could get used to.

But of course, that wore off too. A few weeks after the shove, he went back to his old ways—only this time, by landing an open hand across my face. We'd been out with his friends, and I'd said something he felt was disrespectful. The second we got back to his apartment, the confrontation came. Given that he was a foot taller and at least seventy pounds heavier than me, it really hurt. But worse than the pain was the fear—especially because he wouldn't let me leave. He blocked the door, yelling that I belonged there with him. That I had to take what was coming and accept my lesson about not embarrassing him in front of his friends again.

I fell asleep on his sofa that night, holding a bag of frozen peas to my cheek. When I left for work in the morning, I vowed I'd never return to that apartment again. And of course, his calls started back up that afternoon. He was sorry, he said. He'd had too many beers, he said. Had let his temper get the best of him—but he loved me, would never hurt me, and didn't I know how much I meant to him?

After a few days went by and I still wouldn't pick up his calls, he got Katrina involved. I should have seen every danger sign in the book on that one, but in the end, she was my *sister*. She convinced me I was just being silly and that all couples had arguments. Clearly, Gavin hadn't told her he'd hit me, and I didn't either. I already knew where she stood on the matter.

So, I'd gotten back in the cage.

But I'd done it with guidelines and stipulations, convinced we were playing things by my rules now. If Gavin laid a hand on me in anger ever again, not only would we never see each other, but I would involve the police. And though I had promised my friends I'd spill if he ever hurt me, I never said a word. When we all got together, I kept the conversations light and always redirected the subject to them. Their lives were much happier than mine, and it gave me hope to hear about all their exciting, cheerful plans. Still, Claire had that funny way of looking at a person...and when she directed it at me, I wondered if she could gaze straight down to my soul. It was freaky and frightening but eerily reassuring. She and I had forged some weird, wordless agreement. She knew damn well I was lying but gave my pride the space it needed, always reaffirmed that she was there if I needed her.

And one night, I did...

"Claire? *Claire?* Can you hear me?" I yelled. Or whispered, I wasn't really sure. The noise of the road was so loud, the connection terrible on the grungy old payphone.

"Oh, my God." There were scrabbling noises, as if she was maneuvering her receiver into better position. "Talia?"

"Y-Yeah."

"Honey, where are you? I can barely hear you. Are you okay?"

"N-No." My voice was rough with tears. "I...I need help."

"Anything!" Hers rose with panic. Even with the bad connection, I could hear every strident note of her fear. "Just tell me where you are."

"That's j-just it." A bizarre laugh tumbled out of me. Was I going crazy? Was this even me? "I don't know where I am. He...he..."

"He who?" As swiftly as it had come, her terror vanished. Hardened. Her fury gave me the strength to keep standing. To take another breath. To consider I had a shred of sanity still left in my head. "Gavin?"

"Yes." Silently, I thanked her for saying his name. Right now, I sure as hell wouldn't. "H-He made me get out of his car. I've been walking since then. For forever..." I tried to sound calm, but the cracked sob with which I finished probably gave me away.

"Okay. All right. Breathe, honey. It's going to be okay. Talia, where's your cell phone? This isn't your number." My friend never missed a detail, no matter how small.

"He threw it out the car window." Having to say it made everything more real. I gave in to full sobs, sucking in air when I could. Her concern gave me the permission I needed to fall apart. "I don't know where that is either."

"Are you okay? Physically, I mean. Are you bleeding? Are you hurt anywhere?"

"No. I don't think so. I—I mean he hit me. A bunch of times. I don't think anything is broken. Well, maybe." I sobbed harder. My body ached even when I breathed. I didn't want to alarm her more than she was, but I also couldn't disguise my desperate straits. "I don't know, Claire. Everything...*everything* hurts." And now I wasn't just cataloging my physical damage. I released racking moans between each sentence, knowing I was only making it worse for her to hear me like that.

"Okay. Okay. Breathe again, sweetheart. Try to calm down. Tell me where you are."

A new, teary hiccup. "I—I d-d-don't know!"

"Sssshhh, honey. We can do this. Do you recognize anything around you? Are you still in San Diego? You said you were driving with Gavin."

"Yes." I wiped my running nose with the back of my hand. I started shivering from the cold and the pain.

"Where were you driving from or to?" Her calm voice helped soothe me.

"We were going to his friend's house in Imperial Beach."

"All right. That's good. Did you make it to his friend's house?"

"No. We got into a fight—an argument—on the way there. He was driving like a maniac, and when I said something about slowing down, it made him very angry."

"Do you know what freeway you were on? Look on the phone that you're talking to me on. Is there a phone number printed on it? Are you at a gas station? A grocery store?"

I peered frantically around. "It—It looks like it used to be a gas station, but there's nothing here now. It's abandoned. The number that's printed on the phone is rubbed off. I can't see all the numbers."

"But you can see some of them?" The hopeful rise in her voice encouraged me to look again.

"A few. I can see a few."

"Tell them to me."

"Six, one, nine...and then two, four...maybe a seven...and then I can't see anything but a zero." I banged my head against the phone booth's dirty wall, exhausted even from that effort. "I'm sorry," I blurted. "I'm sorry, I'm sorry, I'm so sorry, Claire. This is all my fault."

"Now stop that, Talia. *Right now.* None of this is your fault, and you know that. But honey...I have to call Killian, okay?"

"No!" I shrieked. "Please, Claire. You can't. No one can know. Gav...he...will kill me if I embarrass him. He told me that when he pushed me out of the car. Please, Claire. *Please.* Just help me, but don't let Killian see me like this. I'm begging you."

There was a heavy sigh from her end. "Honey, you have to listen to me on this. I have to get help. I can't find you on my own; I don't know how—but Killian will be able to do it within minutes. Please let him help you. He'll be discreet. You know he'd do anything for me and for anyone I love. And I do love you, sweetheart. You know that, right?"

I couldn't answer her. I was paralyzed by terror, to the point that nothing but tiny whimpers erupted from my trembling lips. Gavin would hunt me down if he found out. I was certain of it.

"Talia? *Talia.* Be serious. Do you think a weasel like Gavin is a threat to a man like Killian Stone? Do you?" The faith she had in her man was the kind of confidence and loyalty a woman was supposed to have in her spouse. It was admirable and enviable at the same time.

"N-N-No. No. You're right. When you put it like that, you're absolutely right."

"Okay. Thank you. Now I need to tell him what's going on. I'm not hanging up, but I need to go find him in the house, okay?"

"Yes. I'll wait. I've nowhere else to go." I let out another watery laugh, attempting to find a dry spot on my sleeve so I could wipe my nose again. Long, agonizing minutes passed, in which I was tempted to just close my eyes but petrified to even blink.

Finally, *finally,* Claire came back on the line. "Honey? You still there?"

"Yeah." I swallowed hard to keep fresh tears from falling. Her voice was like a window with a candle in the middle of the blizzard I was trudging through. "Yes. I'm here."

"Okay, girl. We'll be there soon."

I choked in sheer shock. "H-How do you know where I am?"

"*I* don't really know, and I'm not sure I want to know, to be honest. But if there's one thing I've learned, when my man sets his mind to something, he makes it happen. Are you warm enough?"

"Not really."

"Where's your coat?"

"Back in his car. My purse too. It was why I had to call collect." My teeth clattered together as if issued a stage prompt. "I can pay you back for the call."

"You'll do no such thing." There was a lot more shuffling from her end of the call now. "Okay, we're in the car, heading to you. Killian has a few guys in route to Gavin as well. We'll get whatever stuff of yours is still in his car, I promise."

"Th-Thank you." All I could do was cry again. I would owe her forever and vowed she'd always know it—but thoughts of all the things I could do to repay her were gashed by an awful comprehension. "Oh God, Claire. Killian's guys. Are—are they going to hurt him?"

"I hope so. Don't you?"

Her voice was matter-of-fact. She was my candle again, only this time, she ignited a whole brick of dynamite inside me.

With the force of that sizzling fuse, I gritted, "Yeah."

"That's my girl."

Somehow, they found me at that abandoned gas station in Imperial Beach—then took me straight to the hospital. I had bruised ribs, a broken nose, and a broken heart, all of which healed over the next six months while I holed up in Killian's amazing penthouse condo in the heart of Chicago. He allowed me to work remotely from there while I nursed my heart and ego back to health before I felt ready to return to San Diego. Everyone was briefed on the story presented to my parents: that I was on assignment for work and simply couldn't be reached. But the truth was, I didn't want to talk to anyone but my girlfriends and my therapist. I was living in a cocoon but in no huge hurry to leave.

Until Killian came to me, lobbing a new assignment into my lap that was too exciting to pass up. Stone Global was getting into the lucrative world of cosmetics, and he wanted me to be the tip of the spear—the contouring brush?—on the marketing ramp-up. It was an ideal assignment in so many ways. Work was the best therapy in the world for me, and this would be a full-time, full-bore, high-dive plunge into a world where I only had to look at beauty and glamour all day...

With only one tiny catch.

Okay, technically, two.

Well, maybe not a catch.

More like...a crazy plot twist. *Very* crazy.

Killian wanted his two closest friends as advisors on the project. A pair of men who gave as much meaning to the term *Roman God* as Killian once had. But while Killian was off the market and permanently in love, his two best friends were still in the game, on all the "hottest" lists, and redefining the words *charming*, *dashing*, and *debonair* on a daily basis.

Drake Newland. Fletcher Ford.

I never thought I'd ever get to speak their names.

To even *whisper* them.

And now, seeing them in the same email "cc" lines as mine...? Surreal barely seemed to cover it.

But Gavin March had only broken my bones. He hadn't broken my spirit. If I didn't at least try to move on with my life, then he would have won. *Unacceptable.*

So I clicked on the "Accept Offer" button—and then got up, stretching to greet one of my last mornings in Chicago, preparing my psyche for the trip back to California.

★ ★ ★ ★

Present Day

Returning home, and back to the current situation, having to listen to my family hail Gavin like he was a favored child or long-lost family friend they were forced to say farewell to against their heart's desire, ate away at the fiber of my very being. But what made the circumstance worse was knowing they would feel the same, even if they knew what had happened between us.

Two things changed the moment I got back to San Diego. I found an apartment of my own and, against my parents' wishes, moved out of my family's home. I also ensured I moved from the neighborhood my parents and all of their friends and relatives lived within. A clean break was necessary, and living on my own in Chicago had given me the confidence to leave the nest in California as well. Taking the job at Stone Global ensured I was making enough money to afford an apartment without a roommate, so a week before Thanksgiving, I had the girls over for our first "girls' night in" to celebrate my new West Coast independence.

I became the consummate workaholic. I spent every waking minute either at the office or doing work from my laptop set up at my kitchen table. The local coffee shop became a second campout spot, where I got to know the baristas on a first-name basis. Drake and Fletcher encouraged me to take less work home and spend more time having fun and doing things with my friends. They said they worried about my intense focus and single-minded drive.

I had never thought of those traits as negatives before, and what they weren't privy to was that they were coping skills that were keeping me from sliding down a very dark rabbit hole, so I stuck with what was comfortable. Turned out denial was a lovely place to visit this time of year.

CHAPTER FOUR

Two weeks after my near nuclear meltdown at my family's Thanksgiving dinner table, Stone Global Corp held its annual holiday party for everyone in the company's sales and marketing departments. Since the company had grown to be so large, Claire and Killian had decided each department should host their own holiday party. Even so, the event was a grand affair, booked at one of the swanky hotels in Mission Valley.

After enjoying a round of wine with some friends, I finally found Margaux and Claire near the bar, though they were both nursing club sodas.

"Did Killian cry?" Margaux taunted her sister-in-law. "He did, didn't he?" She giggled and then burped, which made both Claire and me join her laughter. The early months of pregnancy had both of them glowing in spirit and complexion but queasy in the digestive tracts.

"No. Of course not. He was thrilled! Cautious but thrilled. We both are."

Margaux scoffed. "You're just protecting him. I know that pussy brother of mine cried like a girl when you told him. Fuck it; I'll ask Alfred. That valet can't keep a secret to save his life. Well, unless you're asking him how he makes those lattes I love. *That* he won't tell me for anything." Margaux rolled her eyes dramatically, but we all knew she was serious. When it came to creamy milk and coffee, the woman didn't mess around.

"Who cried like a girl? And about what?"

As we spoke of the devil, he appeared at his wife's side. As soon as Killian was within reach of Claire, he had his arms around her with protective tenderness, as always. I watched them whenever I was around, probably looking like a loony stalker sometimes. My fascination wasn't normal, that was for certain. But months in therapy had me painfully in touch with my motivation. I was jealous of their love, plain and simple. Who wouldn't be? Killian worshiped Claire. He would go to battle for his Fairy Queen, even slay a dragon if it came down to it. That man adored his wife, and everyone knew it.

And God, how I craved an epic love just like it.

The woman's laughter broke into my ruminations. Claire was reacting to some crack from Margaux and looked up at Killian as she did, waiting to see how he'd take it. His hearty laugh bellowed through the room, causing half the partygoers to turn in his direction. Of course, when seeing it was just Margaux giving him the business again, people went back to their own conversations, glad to see it was more of the same between the Stone siblings. In short, business as usual.

I smiled and shook my head while sliding onto an empty bar stool. A year ago, if anyone had asked me where I thought I'd be now, it certainly would not have been surrounded by friends and coworkers with so much happiness in my heart, excitement about my job stirring in my belly, and strange and undefinable feelings about my two extremely sexy coworkers in my lady parts...

And as if on cue, Drake Newland slid onto the stool beside me.

That would teach me to use the word *undefinable* about him ever again.

Everything about him was a hundred percent definable,

from the sweep of his powerful presence in the air to the way his dark gaze captured every detail about my hair, my face...and then lower. He smelled incredible, expensive and masculine, and looked even better. His dark-gray suit was cut to accentuate his impossibly broad shoulders, with a wide lapel easily supported by his larger frame. The back of the collar was kissed by the ends of his thick, near-black waves, tamed in place tonight by some kind of pomade that gave them a little shine. Instantly, my fingers itched, coinciding with a fantasy of tangling my hands in those entrancing strands.

"Well, good evening, Mr. Newland," I finally managed to get out, despite how every molecule of air in the immediate vicinity seemed spoken for.

"Miss Perizkova." He hitched up one corner of his mouth, playing along with my let's-be-formal game, while lifting a fresh glass of champagne. Without looking away from my face, he gathered up my hand and wrapped my fingers around the glass. "For you, my lady."

"Oh, ummm...no thank you." Though I seriously couldn't believe I had the fortitude to say it, after his alluringly personal waiter service. "Sorry. It looks amazing. I just really don't think I should have another one. I've had my two-drink maximum already."

Like the devastating, golden yin to Drake's dark and sexy yang, Fletcher Ford appeared as if conjured right out of the air. With athletic grace he needed to have trademarked, the man slid onto the barstool on my other side, his long chiseled legs accentuated by his custom-fit charcoal slacks. He grinned while occupying the empty stool as if daring anyone to *think* about taking it from him, and I felt my lips curling up in response. Was I starting to subconsciously position myself in groups of three furniture pieces these days, or was it just happening by coincidence? *Repeatedly...*

Did it really matter?

Not one damn bit.

"Is two always your maximum?" Drake's sultry grin could melt hearts coast to coast. *Panties too.* Even when smiling, he applied breath-halting intensity to the action. But I'd known that from the moment I'd met him. Like the historical explorer he shared a name with, the man went after every goal with robust focus.

What would it feel like to be the *woman* he focused on?

Okay, now I did need that champagne.

While taking the drink from his hand, I tilted my head in query. "Are we still talking about drinks?"

"And she gets bolder with alcohol. I'm adding that to the notebook." Though Fletcher mumbled it under his breath, I heard him clearly.

I swiveled around on my stool to directly swing my stare up to his, a little shocked by my own brashness but anxious to redirect the spotlight. "Excuse me? Notebook?"

As the man arched one brow over one of his crystal-blue eyes, the brashness left me. There was only molten heat in its wake, and I wallowed in the warmth as he drawled, "Mr. Newland and I believe in taking careful notes about...*projects* we find of value."

I swallowed hard, learning some of the lava was starting to pool in certain places, as Drake leaned in and offered, "You've been a very tough *colleague* to get to know, Ms. Perizkova." Although his nearness allowed his breath to fan across my bare shoulder in a way that felt anything but *colleague*-like.

Heat swelled through my face. Tingled and pushed at

my breasts. Cascaded south, swiftly pooling in the clenching tissues between my legs. An insane giggle burst from my lips. Ohhhh, I *definitely* didn't need more champagne.

"Care to let us in on the joke?" Drake's full smile dissolved the rest of my anxiety. And a few other parts of my body too. I re-crossed my legs, feeling suddenly oversensitive...everywhere. The universe had jabbed my nervous system into some cosmic electric socket, only had forgotten to tell me about it. But it felt good. *Too* good.

Despite the fireworks in my bloodstream, I returned the dark god's gaze and managed to slowly shake my head. At once, Drake's bold features got even more pronounced. His full lips parted before he pressed in at me to grate, "Are you absolutely sure about that?"

"We have ways of making you talk, you know." Fletcher's low whisper came from just inches behind me.

I shifted on the stool again, trying to disguise my widened gaze of intrigue. And curiosity. And arousal. Ohhhh, yes. A heck of a lot of that.

"You like the sound of that."

Somehow Drake's voice got deeper...sexier. As it resounded through me, I swallowed hard and finally fought my way back to uttering, "I...I don't know..."

"Oh, girl. It wasn't a question." He raised one huge hand to the back of my neck. Within seconds, the wattage to my body doubled. Barely suppressing a low moan, I squeezed my thighs together. Trying, with little success, to alleviate the need that bubbled and swelled from inside.

"I—I don't know what you mean." I volleyed my gape back and forth between the two. They were like a perfectly matched set of super spies, the golden charmer and the onyx panther, danger oozing from their every pore. "I mean...you were just joking, right?"

"It doesn't have to be a joke." With his hand still at my nape, Drake casually tilted his beer up to his mouth. I fixed my stare on his deep-pink lips. Goddamnit, those lips. So full. So perfect. So kissable.

I looked from one side to the other. Both men were silent but intent, waiting for my next move. The damn ball was in my court, so to speak.

Oh God, oh God, oh God.

I lifted the flute in front of me and slammed back the remaining champagne as if it were a shot of tequila. Luckily, the DJ announced it was time for everyone to gather in the ballroom for the white elephant gifts. *Saved by the silly office party tradition.* I would have giggled long and loud again if it wasn't so clearly the truth.

"Did you bring a gift?" Drake asked, trailing his big warm hand to the small of my back, steadying me as we left the bar and made our way toward the ballroom's wide doorway.

I turned back to answer. "Maybe. You'll have to wait and see."

"I don't mind waiting." He pressed his fingers tighter to my spine. "To a point."

His growled inflection on the last three words almost made me stop in my tracks. Instead, I managed to recover and query, "Did *you*?"

"Of course." He paused, treating me to that sexy grin again. "The gift is in the giving, lady." He finished his beer and set it on a nearby table as we passed by before adding, "And I suppose that applies for wrapped trinkets too."

I managed a laugh—barely—as we flocked with the herd to

the room in which the shenanigans would take place. "I hope one of you gets mine," I murmured. "I guarantee you won't want to trade it."

"How do you know?" Fletcher grinned down at me, brushing my hair back from my face.

I came to a full stop—as if I could even think of walking while the man was causing a thousand points of lust to cascade through my body—though that instantly caused the couple behind us to collide right into us.

"Ugh, sorry," the guy mumbled. I thought I'd seen him before around the cafeteria.

"Yeah, sorry about that. My shoe. Sorry." I looked down at my nonexistent shoe malfunction, also seizing the chance to toss a playful glower back up at Fletcher. His eyes twinkled like blue diamonds, exposing his full awareness of exactly how his touch had affected me. *All* of me.

Dear God. *This man.* He continued to throw my coordination off. I couldn't walk and chew gum at the same time on a good day. With his potent energy added to the mix, I was hopeless. Stir in a good dose of Drake as well, and I wasn't even at "hopeless" status anymore.

What was I going to do about this? About *them*?

There was always the option of just giving up. Giving in. Being completely honest with myself and admitting how good their touches really felt. How *amazing* it was when they touched me in front of everyone in this room. But a stubborn, hardworking part of me kept stomping her sensible-shoe-clad foot every time I—and they—let our flirtations go a little too far. People in the SGC offices loved to gossip, especially about certain subjects—and that list was topped by the legendary Mr. Ford and Mr. Newland. I refused to be another notch on their bedpost, despite how few would blame me for taking a spin on their merry-go-round of sin. I simply couldn't live with myself if people speculated that my career's success was due to how good I was at the mattress mambo.

Especially with these two.

Especially after what I'd learned about them just a few nights ago.

The alcohol in my system had nothing to do with how I was still reeling from Margaux's revelation at our girls' night gathering. When she'd told me they shared women, it was the biggest news flash—okay, shock—that I had ever heard. How on earth had I not known? I heard the things they said to me, often tag teaming their flirts and innuendos. I just never thought too deeply about it all. Never thought too much about how it would end if I answered *one* of their mating calls. Would one of them gracefully step aside and let the other take me out? That had been my instant assumption. It never occurred, in my wildest wonderings, that they'd seal the deal *together*.

People actually did that?

I had read about a *ménage a trois* in a book once—and was so embarrassed reading the first love scene, I threw the book away in a public park trash can so no one would know it had belonged to me. If a member of my family or neighborhood knew I read something like that, I'd be sent away for "treatment" of some sort. No; it'd be a convent for me, instead of back to school for my master's degree.

Thank God the DJ began the gift game pretty quickly so I could focus on something appropriate and comprehensible. We drew numbers to determine the order in which we would select presents from the table in the center of the room. The fun part of the white elephant exchange was stealing. People with high numbers could take a present from the table or steal a present from someone who had already opened theirs.

Because the Christmas party was only within the sales and marketing departments, the gift price limit was pretty high, at one hundred dollars. Some people bought gag gifts, and some people bought usable gifts. There were a lot of envelopes on the table, likely gift cards or cash. Out of the sixty-four people who attended, I drew number fifty-eight, while Drake had twelve and Fletch had sixty. The process went rather quickly for such a large crowd, with most of the lower numbers opening new gifts. There were a lot of great presents given and a few really ridiculous things. Of course, there were a few sex toys and an apparatus I didn't recognize at all until Fletcher explained what it was.

"People use that to smoke weed." He said it like a quiet secret, which only piqued my curiosity more—and confusion.

"What? Weed? Like unwanted plants in your garden?"

Drake chuckled. "You are so precious, Talia Perizkova." And there he went, with those long, steady fingers at my nape again. "I seriously want to take you home and never let you out of my sight again. Do you even realize that?"

I knew he meant it as a compliment, but I felt defensive. "Why do you say that? What did I say?"

"Many times, it's what you don't say. Your innocence. Your honesty. And fuck...it's all so genuine. It's something one doesn't come across very often. And in our world...the people Fletch and I have to be around most of the time..." For a second, his face tightened as if the secrets in his mind weren't so fun. "Well, it's like finding a diamond in a mud puddle."

His expression didn't change, and I fought against the urge to stroke a hand along the harsh lines of his jaw. Fortunately, I had a valid distraction. "But please...tell me what that thing is." I motioned again toward the device the intern was looking at with adoration. "I really don't understand."

He cleared his throat, evaporating the tension from his features. I didn't mind watching. The column of his neck was corded and strong and burnished and damn near lickable. So much for "distractions."

At last he leaned over and murmured, "Do you know what marijuana is?"

"Of course, I do." My voice came out as a soft screech. He chuckled. I winced. "I'm not *that* naïve."

"That's what Fletcher meant by weed. That's another name for marijuana."

"Ah. I see." I glanced back over to the intern and the small group that had collected near him. "And now that you say that, I've seen that sort of thing before. You put water in the bottom, right?"

"The lady's a quick study." Fletcher put his arm around me and gave a little squeeze—but then kept the position, lightly resting his big hand around the ball of my shoulder.

"Yeah, I remember that from college. My roommate had a very—I'll be kind and call him *adventurous*—boyfriend. His parents made him go home after a semester or two."

Both men laughed and shared stories about "guys they knew" in college that were similarly adventurous, though I had the distinct feeling they were referring to each other with every eye-popping tale. As the exchange continued, they had me alternating between full laughter, disbelieving gasps, and the certainty that many of the stories were embellished just to make me blush.

By the time the gift exchange was over, I ended up with a

gift card to my favorite handbag store at the mall, Drake had a few pairs of ridiculously expensive dress socks, and Fletcher had stolen a set of steak knives from the administrative assistant from the smaller logistics division that supported the sales team. The woman glared daggers at him from across the room until well after the exchange was over.

"You may want to sleep with one eye open tonight, my brother," Drake teased while motioning with his chin to the little opal-haired woman.

"Maybe you should just give them back to her," I suggested. "Clearly she wants them more than you do."

"How do you know she wants them more?" His cocky grin was somehow sexier than his innocent one.

"You're not staring at her the way she is at you." I shrugged, thinking I had made a solid point.

His deep-blue eyes homed in on me. "I can't stare at anyone else when you're in the room, woman."

I almost sputtered out the champagne I'd just sipped. How and when had that gotten there? And why were there a couple of empty glasses next to it, as well?

But first things first. Oh. My. God, I reeled. How much have you had to drink?" I spun toward Drake. "He's not driving, is he?"

"I'm very sober. And being very honest. You look stunning tonight. It's nice to see you in something other than the practical business suits you favor at the office." Although Fletcher's compliment was sincere, I wasn't in the practice of receiving them gracefully.

"Would you rather I wear something like *that* to the office?" I made eyes toward Antonia as she paraded by in her barely there sequined number.

"I have a few ideas regarding what I'd like to see you in." Drake added. "At the office...or otherwise."

"But things like that would never be on the list," Fletcher finished.

"Okaaaayy." I needed to change the subject—about two minutes ago. "So which gifts did you guys bring?"

"That was as smooth as a California freeway." Fletcher chuckled.

"Potholes and all." Drake injected it with an emphasis on *pot*.

I giggled as Fletcher rolled his eyes. I was completely charmed by how they always tried to outwit each other. And more importantly, extremely relieved that we were off the subject of my wardrobe as designed by the two of them.

Fletcher stood taller, clearly proud of the selections he made. "I brought the six-month Wall Street Journal subscription, and Drake brought the hot sauce subscription box."

"Both very popular on the stealing action. Good choices."

"And which one was yours? You were mighty sure of yourself before this all got started, as I recall?"

Somehow, we had found our way to the far corner of the room. I stood with my back against the wall, very grateful for the support of the plaster after one too many drinks. The men were in front of me, a virtual wall of masculinity, blocking the rest of the party from my view. My head spun from the too-loud music and the too-dim lights. The festivities had morphed into a night club vibe, coworkers now bumping and grinding to dance music from current artists no one was even familiar with.

"Sheesh, that last glass of champagne was not a good

idea." I pressed the back of my hand to my forehead. My skin felt clammy in the overcrowded room. Every person I tried to focus on had a double standing just off to the side of them.

"Do you want us to take you home?" Drake stepped in front of me, ducking down to get right in my line of sight.

"No! Definitely not going home with you two." Now I sounded drunk as well as felt it.

"That's not what I said." Damn, his grin was sexy.

"No, of course it's not. Why would you want to do that?" I sounded like a petulant child, even to my own drunken ears.

"Don't put words in my mouth Natalia." Stern-faced Drake was also super sexy Drake. Although hearing him pronounce my full birth-given name was some sort of trigger that made me feel like I was being sent to the naughty corner by my mother.

"How did you know that?"

"Know what?"

"My name."

Was I slurring now too?

"We've been using your name for months. Boy, are you sure your drink wasn't spiked?" He laughed, but I was becoming enraged.

"No. I mean that is my name. My real name. My whole name. My *name* name." And the more I spoke, the bigger of an idiot I was making of myself. "You know what? Forget it. It doesn't matter. I'm going to go. I need to find Claire and Mr. Stone and thank them for the job, I mean for the party. Then go. Yeah, so bye." I waved my hand right in their faces and tried to push past them. With very little effort, they held me in place.

"Let us help you, Talia." Fletcher tried to soothe me, his voice a beautiful ribbon of calm.

"No way." I shook my head sharply, hair sticking to my face when my head stopped moving. And that was the only thing that stopped. The room kept swinging from side to side for a few more ticks of its own metronome. "I know how you two *help* women," I said through a curtain of dark hair.

"What are you talking about?" Drake asked.

"I'm not really as innocent as you think I am. And Margaux told me. About the two of you. *Boy* did she tell me." I clawed the hair from my cheeks and mouth as I spoke.

"Is that right? Can't wait until the next time I see Blondie, then," Drake said more to Fletcher than me.

"You stay away from her." I leaned in closer to let them in on some private information only I knew. "She's *dangerous*," I said in a stage whisper.

Both men burst out laughing, and in my drunken state, I had no idea why. I was very serious with my advice. They could laugh all they wanted, because not only was she rich and gorgeous, she was also pregnant, and if people thought she was mean before, I worried about what those hormones were about to do to that volatile personality.

"I'm not kidding." I stood with my hands on my hips, weaving in the spot my feet were planted.

"No, I'm sure you're not. Come on though; let's get you home." Fletcher wrapped his long arm around my shoulder and tried to tug me toward the door by holding me tightly to his side.

"I told you I'm not going home with you. Or you." I pointed a wobbling finger at Drake.

"We're going to drive you to your apartment, make sure you get inside, and then leave. Nothing more," Drake said in a very businesslike tone.

"Nothing?" Disappointment could be heard in my intoxicated whining.

"Not a thing. Scout's honor." His sexy grin looked nothing like the scouts I remembered from childhood.

"Oh, that's right. You don't want me. How could I forget?" I smacked my forehead with the heel of my hand. Probably much harder than was necessary, judging by the loud noise and multiple looks that resulted from the move.

Drake quickly grabbed my hand before I could let it drop to my side. "I also told you not to put words in my mouth. Did you forget that part?"

"Yep," I said as I twisted my shoulder into his chest, trying to pry my hand from his.

"Try really hard to keep it in this beautiful head." He gave me a quick peck on the forehead where I had just smacked myself before he released my hand.

I stopped in my tracks, halting further movement toward the parking lot. "You think my head is beautiful?"

He stopped and turned to look at me. "I do."

"So do I. For the record," Fletcher called from behind him, having already walked out the door into the parking lot.

"Awww, that's really nice, you guys. You guys are nice. No matter what everyone else says." I started walking again, wrapping my arms around myself when leaving the building. "It's freezing out here."

They laughed again, both putting an arm around each side of me and directing me toward a giant vehicle. When they stopped beside the thing and Drake dug in his pocket for a set of keys I thought he was joking. But then they both made an effort to help me up into the tall truck. "Why didn't you wear a jacket?" one asked, but I couldn't be sure who since I was concentrating solely on my scaling abilities. There were actual steps that appeared from under the side of the vehicle to assist in the climb into the cab.

"Why is this truck so tall?" I asked as I wobbled on my heels, causing both men to keep a careful handle on me until I was inside the truck. "This is silly."

"Because that knucklehead over there was in charge of the car rental this trip, and this is what we ended up with. Fucking Big Foot." Apparently, Fletcher was not impressed with the four-by-four lifestyle.

"It's not that bad. And we get tons of respect on the freeway," Drake defended the vehicle as he got in behind the wheel.

"My B7 gets respect on the freeway," Fletcher snipped.

"But your fancy pants B7 is in Chicago, isn't it? Where I can only assume the shop queen is on her favorite lift at the local BMW dealer?"

"Wow, you two bicker like a married couple," I added from the back seat as I snapped my seat belt into its partner piece.

Again, they threw their heads back with laughter. It made me smile from the inside out. And even though I was intoxicated, I recognized that was something I hadn't done in a long, long time.

"I like you guys." I watched out the window as we pulled out of the parking lot of the Mission Valley hotel. "When this job is over, I'm going to be sad that you leave."

Silence filled the truck's cab. Well, other than the very loud sound coming from the engine.

The whirling sound of the knobby tires on the concrete freeway lulled me to sleep as we drove north. That and the excessive alcohol I drank on a nearly empty stomach made for a bad combo. A gentle hand on my shoulder nudged me awake when we pulled into my condo complex at the outskirts of La Jolla.

"Hey, sleepyhead. We're home."

Fathoms of ocean-blue eyes met my sleepy gaze. Fletcher's face was just inches above mine as he reached across my body to unlatch my seat belt.

"Heeeyyy. I can get that." I smiled dreamily at the beautiful way he cared for me by doing little things.

"I know you can," he murmured back. "I just wanted an excuse to be close to you."

"You don't need an excuse. Don't you know that by now?" I rolled my head around, smiling wider when Drake appeared in my vision as well, his thick dark hair tousled from the sea breeze that stirred the coastal air this time of night. Ohhh, dear Lord. They both loomed in, beautiful and bold, looking like gods and smelling ridiculously good. I bet they felt even better. And right now, with my senses freed and my inhibitions gone, I refused to be a good little girl and keep that from them any longer. "Don't you *both* know that?"

CHAPTER FIVE

"Let's go inside," Drake growled. "If you don't mind, sweet girl?"

Lack of inhibition, still fueled by champagne, allowed natural instinct to take over. I vowed to shut out the voice of self-doubt and her harpy sisters, reticence and anxiety. Tonight, I would allow myself the baser joys in life. Everyone else seemed to take a turn at life's pleasure principles, and mine had finally come. Two of the most handsome men I had ever seen followed me into my apartment like stray puppies followed a child home.

Hopeful excitement strung their bodies tight with sexual energy and need. Mine responded in kind. As soon as my front door was closed and locked, they moved in. Panthers stalking prey, they simultaneously pressed me against the door, one on either side of my body, kissing and nuzzling my skin, licking and nibbling as if they couldn't devour me fast enough.

"Oh God. God yes. Please. Please. So good," I babbled and chanted. Hummed and wordlessly begged for more with the undulations of my body when my mouth was busy with one of theirs. Things were spiraling into a frenzy, and I wanted to savor the experience because I knew this would be my once and done. There would never be an encore of this particular show.

"Guys. Guys. Please. We have to slow down." My words were a mixture of breathy pants and whispered pleas.

"Why? We have all night. We can go all night, baby."

I wasn't sure who answered, since my eyes were rolled back with pleasure.

"Yeah, there's two of us, love. Don't worry about wearing us out, Talia. It doesn't happen." Drake's confidence was sexy and dangerous, promising everything I wanted to hear.

But still, I needed to preserve the memory. "No, I want to remember all of this. I want to savor every second of it and not have a quickie against my front door."

"Okay. Fair enough. Show us where your room is." Fletcher backed away to give me the space to lead them to a more comfortable location.

I grabbed a hand of each and tugged toward the hall that led to my bedroom. They followed willingly, and we fell into a heap on my bed, the old springs protesting the weight of two very big men plus me. The embarrassment only lasted for a second, as I reminded the voices to stop. There was no room for negativity tonight. Only pleasure and brilliance and the magic of bodies coming together as Mother Nature intended.

Against every fiber of my normal weave, I boldly pushed them back on the bed and backed off until I stood before them. They rose up to sitting in unison, the sight funny enough to elicit a giggle from me. They moved so easily together, as if they shared a body and mind. It was magical and creepy all at the same time.

"How long have you two known each other?" I asked, truly curious.

They looked at one another and shrugged.

"Ten years, maybe? Does it matter?" Fletcher inquired, running his fingers through his hair to brush it out of his eyes. The front was longer than the back and tended to flop down over his forehead when it wasn't perfectly tamed with product.

"No, of course not. But I admire your relationship. I wish I were as close with someone as the two of you are with one another. It's a rare treasure. You're very, very lucky." I slipped my fingers under the edge of my sweater and began slowly lifting it up and over my breasts, exposing the black bra I wore beneath. The lacy lingerie was a recent purchase that I was very glad I chose to put on earlier. The matching thong was a real departure from my normal undergarments, and I had been feeling extra sexy all night knowing it was just beneath my skirt.

"It seems like our luck is about to get even better." Fletcher stood and started to move toward me.

"Stop."

And then, "Sit."

My commands halted him in place before he took a step.

He raised his golden brow at my tone but sat back down on the bed. Drake chuckled and nudged him in the side when he returned to his original spot.

"Hopefully you'll think it was worth it." I was losing courage, but again, I shut off the negative voices.

I reached around to the button and zipper of the black pencil skirt I'd paired with my sweater and then opened it slowly. The material slid over my hips and down my thighs into a black fabric heap on the floor. Drake reached forward with an outstretched hand, ever the gentleman, to help steady me as I stepped free of the skirt and stood before them in thigh-high hose, lace thong, and matching bra. The black lingerie blended nicely against my naturally tan skin, and the jewel-embellished pumps I still had on from the party accentuated the muscle tone in my legs. I felt very sexy, and the hungry looks on Drake's and Fletcher's faces made me feel like a million dollars.

"Do you like this?" I swept my closed fingers up and down the length of my torso like a model on a game show when showing the grand prize.

"Definitely." Fletcher nodded.

"Ohhhh, yes," Drake agreed with a resounding rumble.

"Do you want to touch this?" I gave them a tilt of my head this time, rather than the full hand sweep.

This time they answered together. "Yes."

"How badly?" The challenge in my stare is accompanied by my hands on hips.

"Badly." Drake grabbed his swollen crotch through his slacks, his impatience laced with aggression.

His partner's answer was the same. "Agreed."

"Show me." I had no idea where this person I was being had come from, but I was running with it. While it was equal parts exhilarating and terrifying, I wasn't exactly sure what to do now that I had their complete attention. I turned a half turn so they could see my ass in the thong. I didn't have a lot of self confidence overall, but I knew I had a stellar ass.

I stepped one foot to the side, widening my stance by about six inches, and looked back over my shoulder to make sure they were still watching. Mission accomplished. Both of their stares were fixed on my ass, so I straightened up, stood tall again, and turned back to face them.

"I said show me."

They were on their feet in less than a second each, unbuttoning and unzipping their slacks, dropping them around their ankles and trying to kick them off their feet. Of course, neither of them had taken off their shoes first, so they ended up dancing and hopping around trying to get the hem of their pants legs over the end of their loafers. I had to bite my lip to hold in the laugh so I wouldn't ruin the mood.

Finally, they both stood before me, erections straining from their hips in full acknowledgment of my seduction. The power I wielded was intoxicating. I had never understood women who toyed with men and their emotions or hormones. But the allure was becoming clearer by the minute. I had the impression I could get them to do whatever I wanted with the promise of sex at the finish line. It was the "power of the pussy" Margaux always spoke of. It was stronger than the Jedi force indeed. She wasn't making that up after all.

Only there were some major differences between Margaux and me. I couldn't even say the word pussy without turning crimson. How did I expect to employ its mighty power? Time to have some fun with a little role play. I kept chanting in my head, *What would Margaux do?*

"Those are very impressive cocks, gentleman. The dress shirts are distracting me though. Lose 'em." A wave of my finger in the general direction of the white cotton button-downs gave a sassy punch to my command.

They looked at one another as though they were trying to make peace with something.

"Is there a problem?" I barked.

"No. Well, actually, yeah. I didn't quite expect this... this...dominant attitude from you," Drake admitted while unbuttoning his shirt. His defined torso nearly stole my breath when I finally laid my eyes on it in its naked glory.

"Jesus, Mary, and Joseph. You are beautiful." There was no chant or role play reminder that would've kept me from appreciating the man's physique.

"Do you like this?" He mimicked my motion from earlier with a very sexy grin.

"I do. You. Are. Perfection." I was tempted to wipe my chin in case drool had dribbled down from my gawking.

"Oh my God. Don't say things like that to him. His ego has already petitioned for its own zip code. Don't add fuel to the fire, hon." Fletcher swiped his rolled-up shirt at Drake's abdomen.

My attention was refocused on Fletcher when he spoke. His body was equally stunning, although very different. Long, lean muscle, defined at every dip and dent of his frame, making it difficult to not stare.

"Wow. You too?" I finally found a few words. "How is this possible?"

"Me too what?" He forgot what the subject was during his locker room antics with his best friend.

"Perfection. How do you two do this? I know how much you work. How do you keep your bodies looking like this?"

"We both play water polo, and that's very vigorous. We try to eat well, we drink occasionally, like tonight but it's not a big part of our routine, and we hit the gym when we can." Fletcher smiled as he spoke, watching me stare as he tossed his shirt aside. "Now, can we come closer to you? Touch you?"

"One of you can. You decide which one." Time to regain control.

"What will the other one be doing?" Drake asked.

"Watching, of course." This time it was my turn to shrug, as though the answer was so obvious.

They both groaned but immediately turned toward one another and began negotiating who would have the first chance to touch me. They quickly parted and faced me, Drake sat back on my bed, and Fletcher prowled toward me.

"Stop." My arm was outstretched fully.

"What? You said..." His pouty sulk was ridiculously sexy too. These two men did sexy like Baskin-Robbins did ice cream, in thirty-one flavors.

"I just want to look at you one more time. All of you."

"Have you seen a naked man before?" He was definitely surprised at the possibility that I hadn't, but not condescending if it had been the case.

"Not one this glorious. That's for sure." I was completely fascinated.

"Wait. You aren't a virgin, are you?" Then came the panic I would've expected from men with their experience.

"No. I'm not. What would give you that idea?" I thought I was playing the take-charge roll pretty well.

Guess not.

"Okay. Good." His shoulders visibly lowered as the relief settled in.

"Would that matter?" Now I was genuinely curious.

"Well, yeah, I think it would."

"Why?"

"I just think we would handle things...differently." He looked over his shoulder to meet a nod of agreement from his buddy.

"That's interesting. But not for us to worry about right now." An oddly curious part of me wondered what losing one's virginity would be like with these two. My own experience was so unremarkable—more like regrettable. I wished I could replace it with something meaningful.

"Agreed." Fletcher took another step toward me, and I put my hand up again. This time, he completely ignored my command, grabbed my outstretched hand, and pulled me flat against him so forcefully our flesh slapped when we collided.

"No more playing around, young lady," he spoke against my lips.

"Who's playing?" I had just enough time to answer before he kissed me.

Roughly.

Fabulously.

Then, "I want to feel you against me. Feel your silky skin under my hands, this hair through my fingers. These lips under mine." With each description, he made the motion. His hands roamed across my collarbones, and then he flattened his palms over my breasts and up and over my shoulders. He sifted his fingers through my hair, tugging my head back and lighting up the millions of nerves in my scalp. And finally, he covered my mouth with his lips again, kissing and then exploring deeper with his tongue when I opened enough to allow him access.

A deep moan filled the room, and I knew our witness was enjoying the display. An answering moan escaped Fletcher's throat, filling mine and then the air when I released my breath.

"Okay so far?" He was checking in on my welfare, which should've been sweet but instead irked me.

"Yes. So good. Why wouldn't I be? You don't have to be careful with me, Fletcher. I'm not fragile." I tugged on his face so he would meet my stare. "I'm serious. I want you two to treat me the way you would any other woman you take home for a night."

"No." He shook his head vehemently. "We want to treat you like you're special, Talia. You *are* special to us." Kisses followed his words down my neck and back to my mouth, barely giving me a chance to respond.

"Don't do that. Don't say pretty little lies because you think I'm a delicate bird. I'm not. I want you to use me, Fletcher. Like you do other women."

He pulled his head back so I couldn't distract him with more kissing. "Is that what you think we do?" His blue eyes had darkened like the Midwestern sky before a summer thunderstorm. The color was so transformative it was fascinating.

"Isn't it?" Why had the truth upset him? They were the known players here, not me.

Still, he looked like I'd just kneed him in the groin instead of given him a free pass at a wild night of sex. I was so confused. And clearly a terrible seductress. But I continued to go for broke.

Leaving Fletcher where he stood, I climbed onto the foot of my bed on my hands and knees and slowly crawled to the center. I kept the slope of my back low, ensuring my ass stuck out high in offering. Drake swiveled in the place where he sat, reaching for me as I crawled behind him. He stroked up the back of my thigh and teased the tips of his fingers along the edge of my thigh-highs. Over and over, he repeated the motion until I thought I would scream if he didn't touch me somewhere else. Fletcher had come over to the bed but stayed standing alongside it, stroking his erection while watching Drake tease me. I hung my head between my shoulders and moaned in frustration.

"Talia?" Fletcher's voice was low and husky with need.

I looked up, almost poking myself in the eye with the head of his dick as he held it in front of my face.

"Suck me." Simple words, spoken so easily. Froze me.

"Is there a problem with that?" Drake asked, noticing my

body language before Fletcher.

"N-N-No. No." I wasn't about to tell them that I was the world's worst blow job giver, and my ex used to ridicule me into doing it and then criticized my performance until I left the room crying.

No way! That was definitely not what Margaux would do.

I reached for Fletcher's cock and was almost stunned by how hard it was in my fist. Apparently, Gavin was both small and semi-hard. *Loser*. I smiled to myself and went for it with gusto. I gave Fletcher the best, most enthusiastic blow job I could possibly give. I paid attention to every single inch of his beautiful cock, every side, every nook and cranny. I cradled his balls in my hand and squeezed carefully, and when he moaned or made a sound indicating he liked what I was doing, I did it more.

Drake kept busy toying with me while I pleasured Fletcher. It was amazing. The better I felt, the more I wanted to give to Fletcher. There wasn't a single time I thought, *Oh my God, this is never going to end* like I did the entire time I was with Gavin. In fact, I could barely think at all because Drake's fingers were very skilled. He had me so worked up by the time he finally moved my thong to the side and touched me directly on my bare folds, I thought I would have an orgasm instantly. I jerked so violently, Fletcher quickly pulled back.

"Dude, a little warning next time," he reprimanded his friend with a playful smirk on his lips.

"I didn't do anything." Drake barely looked away from what he was doing long enough to address Fletcher's concern.

"Well, something just almost made me a member of the John Bobbitt club."

"Our girl's just a bit high strung at the moment, isn't that right, Talia?" He flicked his thumb directly over my clit to prove his point. I yelped from the sensation, wanting to smack him for taunting me so mercilessly.

"You're driving me crazy with all the teasing!" I barely recognized my own voice through the whining.

"Yeah, but how wet are you right now?"

I could feel the blood rush to my face from embarrassment before I could channel my brash friend.

"Well?" Drake repeated.

"Very," I finally whispered, even though I meant for it to come out loud and proud.

"Show Fletcher."

Before I could think better of it, I reached between my legs and ran my fingers through my arousal. Then, I brought the same hand back up in front of Fletcher's face to show him the sticky dew between my fingers.

"He wasn't kidding, was he?" Mischief made his blue eyes more like the island waters of the Caribbean now. But two could play at the mischief game.

I reached for his erection still standing at attention between us and painted the moisture from my fingers up and down his shaft. Keeping eye contact with him as long as possible, I moved back down and slid his cock deep into my throat, tasting myself on his shaft as I did so.

"Damn it, girl." He fisted his hands into my long hair on either side of my head, controlling my movement.

The feeling of tension against my scalp somehow thrilled me. More so, the idea of him feeling so out of control from the pleasure I was giving him that he had to take over before he lost it completely. Drake timed his penetration perfectly, sliding two fingers into my soaked hole at the same time Fletcher grabbed on to my hair. Unwittingly, I moaned loudly around his full shaft, causing another string of curses to erupt from Fletcher.

"D! Man! We work together! No?" Fletcher's voice was filled with agony.

"It's her. I'm telling you. It's her. She's so unexpected." I felt his deep chuckle in bursts of hot breaths against my ass cheek and then the rasp of his dark stubble as he rubbed his cheek against mine. A moment of panic shot through me when I realized how close his face was to all of my...well...things. Instinct reared its head and had me pulling away from Drake as though he had just stuck me with a pin. I had issues with a man having his face down there. But again, today was not a day for hang-ups. I didn't want to explain any of my silly insecurities to these two, and I didn't want to risk ruining what would likely be the best experience of my life, so my panic snowballed, doubled-down, and kicked up a notch, all at the same time.

While they clearly noticed my internal battle, they were patient and respectful and gave me the few moments to reorganize my thoughts and get back into the game.

With another check-in on my welfare, Drake stroked my hair away from my face. "Are you okay, baby? Please be honest. Neither one of us will ever pressure you to do something you're not comfortable doing."

"No. It's fine. I'm fine. Please, forget all that. I have a few hang-ups, but seriously, I don't want to worry about any of that right now. Okay? Can we just drop it?"

"Are you sure?" Fletcher asked from where he still stood beside my bed, beautiful erect cock in his fist.

"Positive." My stare focused intently on his fingers and how they worked his flesh in an almost vise-like grip.

"Perfect. Now finish what you started with Fletcher. He looks like he's about to burst, no? Swallow if you're into that. No worries if you're not." He shrugged nonchalantly. "See how easy we are?"

And with that, Drake returned to fingering my pussy but was deliberate in keeping his face closer to mine while doing so.

Fletcher fisted his cock while watching me enjoy Drake's attention. When I finally checked back in to the situation, he offered his stiff shaft to me, and I gladly took him into my mouth and drove him to orgasm. I worked his shaft with my hand in rhythm with my sucking to give his whole length attention. Right before he was ready to explode, he groaned out a warning. "Talia. Talia, I'm going to come. Move if you don't want a midnight snack, baby."

Driven by the new, more daring side of my persona, I sucked harder, pumped faster, and apparently, turned him on the last bit that was needed to finish him off. He held my face still and thrust his hips forward one last time, and I felt the warm fluid spurt from his shaft into my mouth. I swallowed several times, enjoying the taste and the experience, feeling closer to him, even if that was probably silly. Whether I was pretending to be someone I wasn't or not, deep inside, I was still naïve me, and that experience meant something to me. It would probably haunt me later, but some things you just couldn't pretend *not* to be, no matter how hard you tried.

I didn't have too long to get caught up in my own head. A quick tug back on my hips landed me solidly in Drake's lap, his impressive erection nudging my backside. He nuzzled my hair and wrapped his arms tightly around my waist.

"You smell so good. I don't know if it's your shampoo, or

your perfume, or all of it together."

"I don't think it matters. I just don't want to stop smelling it." Fletcher reclined against my headboard and stretched out his long legs. They seemed even longer in my queen-sized bed with the three of us on it at the same time. He stretched his arms out to me, and Drake stood, still holding me with his arms around my waist, and deposited me in the open space between Fletcher's legs. Fletcher quickly arranged me so my back was against his chest and my legs were stretched out on the inside of his. I fit inside there perfectly.

When I commented as such, Drake got a wolfish smile. "I like that idea. Let's see how I fit inside you. Shall we?" He was stroking his hard cock, preparing it for the condom he held in his other hand. I watched with rapt attention, utterly fascinated by both watching him handle himself and how unashamed they were about their sexual needs.

The pressure of Drake's cock at my entrance brought my attention back to what was happening in the present. He pressed in slowly, allowing my body time to adjust to his. My pussy was soaked and swollen with need, and I wanted to freeze the memory of his stunning face looking down at me, twisted with concentration and need, forever.

"Damn, you're tight. You sure you've done this before? Please don't lie about something so important." His voice rasped with craving.

"Yes. I'm very sure. It's just been a while, that's all."

"Okay. I'll try to go slow." He had a pained look on his face as he said it.

"Please don't. It really feels good." I grabbed on to his tight ass and pulled him into me. He was able to maintain control of the pace even with me trying to take over, but it did bring out the sexiest grin I may have ever seen. Drake Newland had the most sinful pair of lips I think the angels ever bestowed upon a man. They were deep red and very full, and the urge to bite into one of them was nearly impossible to fight.

"What on earth are you thinking? It looks devilish, whatever it is." He slid a bit farther in, the fullness becoming almost too much to handle.

"Probably would get me in trouble if I acted on it."

"Oh yeah? It may be worth it, then."

He was goading me, and it made it even more tempting. He was also nearly all the way inside me, his body hovering just a few inches over mine as he supported much of his weight. With his best friend cradling my body from behind, I was in the most enviable position a woman could be in. Fletcher toyed with my breasts each time Drake rose off me. He stroked my arms and neck and even my ears when he couldn't. As long as he was touching me, everything seemed perfect.

"You guys," I moaned. "This is heavenly. So perfect. It feels so perfect being between the two of you."

"I'm glad we could bring you pleasure, Talia," Fletcher whispered between strokes and kisses.

"Yeah, a girl could really get used to this." I sighed in return, trying to forget that after tonight it would never happen again.

Drake kissed me again, but it was so deep, it was like he was crawling inside my soul. As though he wanted to become a part of me. Almost as much as I wanted to be a part of him. Of them.

"Can you feel me, baby? Deep inside you?" He moaned, voice so deep it vibrated through me.

"I do. I do." I arched my back, pressing my breasts into his chest, not wanting any space between us.

"I. Could. Stay. Here. Forever. Never. Leave." He thrust in and out, keeping time with his lovely words.

"Mmmmm yes. So good, Drake. So good." I could've wept, the pleasure was so intense.

"I need to come, Talia. I need to come deep inside you. Fill you."

"Do it. Give me everything, Drake. It feels incredible. Fuck me. Fuck me harder. Yes. Yes. So good." I shouted my release along with his, and then he collapsed on Fletcher and me and panted for a minute or two while we calmed down.

★ ★ ★ ★

I must have drifted off soon after, because the next memory was waking the following late morning in my own bed. I wore the same clothes I'd worn to the party, and my shoes were lined up neatly beside my bed. My phone was plugged in on my nightstand, and my car keys were beside it. Heaven help me if I drove home, because I had no memory of doing so. I was normally a very light drinker, and on the rare occasion that I overindulged, I took a cab or Uber home.

A quick scan of the empty but neatly made bed beside me crushed my heart and made me dash for the bathroom. If I got sick now it would serve me right. First, drinking so much was downright foolish, especially at a work function. Second, thinking those two men had any interest in me outside of my own dreams was ridiculous, and I deserved a solid crash into reality.

Luckily the nausea passed, and I was saved from offering a prayer to the porcelain gods. A second glance at my half-made bed as I passed my bedroom on the way to the kitchen was another check mark on the long list of why I needed to stop day dreaming about Drake and Fletcher and all the unmentionable things I'd like to do with them that would have HR filling out my exit interview faster than Margaux could get to a tag sale at Saks.

Who was I kidding? She never waited for things to go on sale. That was my lot in life. Definitely not hers.

I went to the kitchen for some coffee and found the bottle of Motrin and a hand-written note from Fletcher.

Wait. Fletcher? Fletcher was in my apartment?

It all came back to me as I read his stunning swirled handwriting. They'd brought me home and tucked me in. My car was in my designated parking space, and my keys were on my nightstand. They looked forward to seeing me at the office on Monday. No wonder I'd had a sex dream about them. They were in my bedroom. They'd put me in my bed. Oh my God. How would I face them at the office after acting so unprofessionally? This was all Margaux's and Claire's fault for putting the sex nonsense in my head the other night when they were at my house.

Thank God it was all a dream. But still...I had to survive an entire trip with them in less than a week, and now I'd be so wound up every time I saw them, even worse than I usually was.

I wanted to crawl back into bed, pull the covers over my head, and forget the whole mess ever happened. Actually, that was a perfect idea. I made a cup of coffee, took two pills, and went back to bed. I put my phone on do not disturb and pretended to disappear for the rest of the day.

CHAPTER SIX

My rolling luggage beat a steady *click-click-click* on the pavement breaks as I walked up to the VIP security checkpoint at the terminal of San Diego's Lindbergh Field. I knew this trip would be a turning point in my career, but a funny feeling nagged at the back of my mind, predicting it would be more than just that.

I'd been feeling stagnant for a while, wanting so desperately to move forward but remaining anchored in the same place. This trip, while only a few days, was the change I needed. Christmas had come and gone, and the cosmetics line was finally ready to take flight, and consequently, so were we—to launch the new line and all its products at Cosmetics Con, the internationally attended trade show that took place each year in the City of Sin. What better place to get out of a funk than nonstop Las Vegas?

The team, consisting of Drake, Fletcher, and me, was taking SGC's corporate jet from San Diego to Las Vegas. A thirty-five-minute flight would put us right in the middle of the bright lights of the neon Strip in the Mohave Desert. I'd been to Vegas a few times before with my family—Aunt Sarafina's fondness for dollar slots was the stuff of jokes for us all—but I had a feeling this trip would be very different from hanging out with my parents, siblings, and extended family.

That premonition didn't have a thing to do with my travel mates.

Okay, maybe a *little* something.

Drake Newland.

Fletcher Ford.

Oh, God.

It was all Claire's and Margaux's fault. They were the ones responsible for the anxiety practically eating me alive. We'd had a girls' night just before Thanksgiving at my place, and once they learned I was taking this trip with Drake and Fletcher, the taunting advice and playful jabs had begun in full. They'd teased me with all the love in their hearts, but I still couldn't erase their words from my frontal lobe.

Those two can smell a girl like you coming a mile away. That was the only G-rated dig I could recall. By the end of the night and after a good amount of Patrón, I had been getting advice on what lingerie to pack—and *not* to pack. I was certain my usually olive-colored skin had gone three shades of rose after that one, but Claire and Margaux were good at doing that to me on a regular basis. I hadn't been sure if they had been truly serious or just trying to see how crimson they'd been able to make me.

Also adding to my nerves this morning... Memories of the night of our company's Christmas party, drinking way more than I thought I had and needing an escort home, complete with personal tuck-in service by the aforementioned travel mates.

Followed by a very explicit dream involving said travel mates that even now had my temperature rising beneath my well-thought-out ensemble.

"Good morning, Miss Perizkova. You look lovely today."

I glanced up at the uniformed steward who appeared just as I cleared security, not quite sure how to react.

"Stop flirting with my girl, Martinez."

As the man chuckled, heat crept across my cheeks. Fletcher Ford appeared by my side, swiping my rolling bag before it left the TSA belt. The SGC board member, innovator, and creative taskmaster—not to mention dead-on Justin Timberlake lookalike—who'd helped start up this new wing of the company fell into step with me while we headed toward our flight.

"Mr. Ford." I tried to give his physique, perfectly fitted in Armani today, as discreet a onceover as I could. "Good day."

"Well, it's a good day *now*," he murmured in return.

Time for a new subject. Pronto.

"I can handle my own bag, thank you."

I snatched at my roller.

He moved the luggage just out of my reach. "Darling, I'm sure you can handle a lot of things for yourself, but would it kill you to allow me to be a gentleman now and then? Come on. Let all of my mama's hard work do some good." He laid on the killer smile that had earned him the devil's own reputation.

My resistance turned to dust. "Where's Drake? Err, I mean Mr. Newland?"

And I'd asked that...why? The two men made me almost speechless when I was with them one-on-one. When they were together, which was damn near all the time these days, I became a bumbling fool. I should've been grateful for the reprieve.

Fletcher smiled again—though this time a bit of sadness seemed to flicker in his blue eyes. "What's wrong? You don't like *just* me?"

"That's not what I meant at all." Now I felt like an idiot. "Really, I didn't—"

He put me out of my rambling misery with a steady hand on my forearm. "Easy, Tolly. I was just yanking your pretty chain."

"Why do you call me that?"

"What? Tolly? It's your name, isn't it? Talia?" He said my full name more dramatically—before adding that damn grin again.

Thankfully, we were nearing the plane and I could get away from the uneasiness of having to worry about witty chit-chat. While we were interacting professionally, I could hold my own, but this personal stuff was so far out of my league. I was never really good at it with normal guys, let alone a smooth, gorgeous god like him.

He opened the door to the tarmac, and the San Diego sunshine instantly warmed me. A grin spread across my lips. We were having one of the mildest winters I could remember, and it was wonderful. I really loved living in Southern California.

"Of course," I finally answered him. "I've just never been called anything but Talia."

"Maybe it's time for things to change then, hmmm?" He nodded toward Stone Global's private jet, sleek and white, waiting across the pavement. "And there's the *other* subject of your wonderment—already getting on board the plane, I see."

I followed his line of vision to the top of the jet's entry stairs, where Drake Newland was ducking his tall frame to fit into the doorway. His short hair was spiked in its usual perfect fashion, his tight, muscular body molded into his custom-fit dress shirt.

Not that I noticed the fit of his clothes.

Okay, I noticed. But it was hard not to—with either of these men. They were tall, handsome, and very well-defined.

I'd been working with them on the development of the cosmetics line at SGC for many long months, over many long hours. I would have had to have been dead not to notice their jaw-dropping physical appeal.

And their flirtatiousness.

Oh, yeah. That.

As in, flirtatiousness. All the time.

In the beginning, I'd told myself they simply behaved that way around all females, until Claire and Margaux insisted that wasn't the case. It hadn't been long before Taylor Matthews, my girlfriend from the sales department, had added her own agreement to that theory. After that, I'd begun to watch Drake and Fletcher a little more closely. For research purposes only, of course.

And what had that research told me?

At the moment, the only female I could pinpoint their pulling out all the blatant charm and urbane behavior around for...was me.

So what did I want to do with that recognition?

I had no idea.

The truth of it thrilled me.

But really, it terrified me.

★ ★ ★ ★

We were airborne and on our way in short order. The stress of the project's culmination, as well as the importance of the task ahead of us this weekend, was catching up with me in the form of a tension headache. Luckily this smaller of the two Stone Global jets was as luxuriously appointed as the large one, allowing me to rest my head on a plush cushion of the sofa while we climbed to our cruising altitude.

The men were bent together over some documents at the galley table across the aisle, engrossed in a debate regarding whatever they were reading. Both Drake and Fletcher were passionate about everything they did, a fact I'd quickly learned over the months we'd been working together, although each man expressed his drive so differently.

Drake Newland was quiet and somewhat brooding, but if an issue came to a head, he turned into an erupting volcano. He'd simmer beneath the surface for a long period, not giving anyone an indication of his thoughts, until he finally blew—often with catastrophic results. But that also translated to his unadulterated enjoyment of life, which he grabbed with the same gusto. He loved his family with a fervor that matched my affection for my own. On a number of occasions, I'd been guilty of eavesdropping on his phone calls to his sister, brother, and even his mom. It made me happy to hear people who still valued family the way I did.

Fletcher Ford was a huge contrast. He always and immediately voiced every single thought running through his head, telling you what he believed, whether good, bad, or indifferent. He laughed a lot more than Drake, but it was deceiving. He had a distinct pit of sadness in him, just under the surface. I wasn't sure where that stemmed from, but he dipped into it on a regular basis. Fortunately, he bounced back from the darkness easily. At least, most times.

"Tolly?"

I recognized Drake's deep voice, even with my eyes closed. Great. He was in on the nickname now too.

"Hmmm?" I kept my head back, not opening my eyes.

"Are you thirsty? Hungry?"

"No, thank you."

"Are you sure?" Fletcher chimed in now.

"Why are you two playing mother hen?" I chuckled but still didn't open my eyes.

"You're quiet," Fletcher explained. "You haven't talked to us. Or even opened your eyes."

"What's wrong?"

I sighed. There was no point in blurting out how I was so stressed about the cosmetics division launch being a gigantic failure, thereby dragging my career down the pipes right behind it, not to mention being closed into this tiny tube of a plane with two incredibly hot men. No point, and no method. There simply wasn't a tactful way to broach either subject.

"Nothing's wrong. I'm just a little tense, and I'm working on a headache. No worries."

Suddenly, the sofa dipped on both sides of me. My eyes shot open, and I bolted upright, all notion of relaxing gone. Drake sat to my left, Fletcher to my right. Both their chairs had been pushed out and left in a flurry. And I hadn't heard one damn second of their movements. Well, that settled it. The bastards had to be part ninja and part cat.

Without a word of warning, Fletcher grabbed my hands between his large, warm ones. "Why are you tense? What's wrong?"

"Oh, sheez." My ire was gawky and fake, even to me. "I already told you—"

"It's not the launch, is it? *Talia.* We have this nailed. You know that, right?"

"Fletcher, really—"

"You've been working too hard." Over my head, he made eye contact with Drake. "I told you she's been pushing herself too hard. We should've sent her home earlier."

Drake pushed in closer. "Turn around. Let me rub your shoulders."

Holy...wow. I felt the heat coming off his hard, huge body like microwaves. I literally pictured waves floating from him to me...and it was intoxicating.

The effect was intensified when mixed with the warmth of Fletcher's hands. He still held both of mine, though he had begun to stroke from my wrists to fingertips with slow, caressing motions.

"Let Drake rub you." His voice dropped in volume...and by several octaves. "We can help you relax."

So soft. So seductive. My heartbeat quickened. I was flustered that Fletcher might feel my excitement through my pulse if he kept touching my wrist. But when I tried to pull back, he held me tighter.

"What are you two up to?" I couldn't help but be skeptical. We were work associates. Suddenly, this *really* didn't feel like work.

"You've been overworking, and it's our fault." Drake's voice was quieter too. "We should've taken better care of you. Let us do that now."

Ohhhh boy, these two were dangerous. My belly flip-flopped with—I didn't even know what. I'd never felt like this in my entire life, and nothing had really happened other than one man stroking my hands while the other massaged my shoulders. It felt...good. And nice. So very nice...

Every single warning bell of self-preservation pealed through my brain.

"Listen. Your jobs aren't to take care of me. I'm a grown woman. I can take care of myself. It's nothing some Motrin and a nap won't fix."

"Talia."

Something about the way Drake said my name, with that particular cadence and tone, made me forget all the reasons I should fight the notion of them taking care of me and just let it happen.

"Okay," I relented. "So a shoulder rub would probably feel pretty great."

"Good girl." It was a low, satisfied sound that brought a new flurry of tingles through strange places in my body. "Can you move your hair out of the way?"

Without waiting for me to reply, he gathered my hair in his thick fingers, twisted it into a ponytail, and handed the rope over my shoulder. I held the end while he started kneading my shoulders.

Fletcher took the ponytail from me, a dazzling smile lifting his generous lips. "Now, just relax. After all, I've wanted to feel your hair for so long. Now I have an excuse. *Relax*, Tolly. Let Drake work his magic."

Drake let out another rumble. It was deeper this time... damn near a masculine sigh. "We should be ashamed of ourselves, brother."

My head shot up. "You guys are brothers?"

Fletcher turned on the lethal version of his smile. "In the ways that matter. But no, not blood relatives. Now close your eyes and relax." His next comment went to Drake. "Why are we ashamed of ourselves this time?"

"She has knots worse than I've ever felt. I'll bet at least half this shit is because of SGC." He dipped his head, brushing my nape with his next words. "Why doesn't your boyfriend rub these out at night, little Tolly?"

Gone was the growl. Now his voice was a guttural hum, joining with the magic of his hands to unarm me of the natural instinct against his fishing expedition. Down I fell into his trap, like the naïve girl they were convinced I was.

"I don't have a boyfriend. And my turtle refuses to do anything for anyone but himself. Selfish bastard."

They both laughed. I rarely joked. About anything. I was always of the mindset work was for, well, working. Not goofing off.

Fletcher continued massaging my hands, kneading my forearms as well as my wrists and fingers. All of the daily abuse from using a computer and mouse suddenly flowed out of my muscles and nerves, turning me into a bowl of Jell-O.

I was in heaven. They both worked quietly, tirelessly, relieving my exhausted body, moving from one side to the other, eradicating the tension that had accumulated in my muscles and tissues. In that moment, I would've told them any secret I knew, confessed to any crime I'd never committed, agreed to any wild hypnotic suggestion, if only they'd continue.

I was on the verge of falling asleep when Fletcher gently laid my hair back over my shoulders. I rested my head on the sofa again, a smile spread across my face...or at least I thought so. I would thank the men in a few minutes, after I enjoyed the glow a while longer.

All too soon, the pressure in the plane shifted. I could feel our descent, especially as my ears popped. I would've loved the massage to go on for hours, now that I'd accepted a rational excuse about why they had touched me like that. They were right—we'd all been working so hard, and it wasn't such a big deal that they just wanted to take care of me for a bit. No harm, right? Coworkers cared for one another. That was what teams did. Made them stronger.

That's a load of shit, and you know it.

So the minute—the *second*—the plane landed in Vegas, this taking care of one another would be back on the inappropriate list. While we were in the air, no one would be any wiser.

When I finally cracked open my eyes, the men were back at the table, leaning toward each other once again. They were already so deep in conversation they didn't notice I'd even looked. Still feeling limp and lazy, I slid my eyes shut, resting while we made our way toward McCarran.

"Where do we go from here?" The quiet rasp belonged to Fletcher.

"We still follow her lead," Drake rumbled. "She had a hard time just letting me rub her shoulders. But my God, touching her was a fucking dream come true. She's perfect."

"I hear you. Her hands...they're so soft."

"And she smells *really* good."

Fletcher whispered, "Yeah. Reminds me of mornings at that cabin we used to go to in the mountains. Clean and crisp and—damn, I don't know. Sure as hell made my dick stand at attention. Not like it dooon't always when she's around."

"No shit. Thought I'd have to hit the head before we landed. Luckily, things settled down."

I swallowed hard and focused on breathing right. Was I really hearing this? They'd definitely flirted over the past few weeks, but this was more than I thought I'd ever hear from these two men—about *me*.

A memory flashed, clear and stunning, of Margaux's claims about the way they had sex with women. They liked doing it at the same time! *No.* Just...no, no, no. I couldn't do something like that. But apparently, I could dream about it just fine. And maybe I could also revisit said dream a few hundred times in my daydreams since then. But...if I ever did do something like sleep with two men at the same time, if my family ever found out, I'd be the disgrace of our entire bloodline. Black sheep? I'd be the black *elephant*. At the very least, I'd be disowned.

This one—these *two*—would have to be passed over.

But what if their massage was just a little appetizer of what things could be like...of what it felt like to go to bed with two men at the same time? With *those* two men, a girl just might die from pleasure overload. Fletcher and Drake would definitely pile on the enjoyment too. Their hands alone were skilled, magical...and likely just the tip of the iceberg when it came to their bedroom prowess.

The sofa dipped again, but I really didn't want to face them after what I'd just overheard. I focused on not moving. After a moment, I felt the seat belt being fitted and clicked into place around my lap. I gave up the fight and opened my eyes. Fletcher was leaning over me, his face no more than six inches from mine. Blue eyes. Proud jaw. Luscious lips. The man was intoxicatingly handsome.

"Thank you." The whisper popped out, almost of its own volition. Well, I'd been raised to have good manners—just not to deliver them in a rasp worthy of a porn star. But what the hell. We *were* still on the plane, which meant all of this still didn't count. And I was really grateful to him...for so much more than helping me relax during the flight.

Again, Mr. Sexy broke out the smile that would melt a nun. "That wasn't so hard, was it?"

"What are you talking about?" My voice was sleepy, helping with the keep-things-casual angle. Hopefully.

"Letting me take care of you a little bit."

"Well, you were right. It wasn't hard. The massage was wonderful. And you too, Mr. Newland."

I didn't have to look to know Drake's eyebrows jumped. "Mr. Newland?"

"My headache is completely gone." Ignoring him was probably the best strategy. "That really was the best massage I've ever had."

"We're happy to be at your service whenever you need it, beautiful."

I went ahead and rolled my eyes. "You guys lay it on pretty thick, don't you think?"

Suddenly, there was a powerful finger beneath my chin. Then Mr. Newland's storm-filled gaze consumed my vision.

Past tight lips, he stated, "We're not *laying* anything on, girl. We mean every single word we say." A pulse jumped in the center of his hard jaw. "We may be a lot of things, Talia, but bullshitters isn't on that list. I'll thank you not to make that mistake again."

Just as quickly, he released me. Rose to his full, imposing height. Stomped his way to the small door leading into the bathroom.

"I think I made him angry," I mumbled.

Fletcher clasped my hand again. "He has issues with being called a liar."

"Yikes. I guess so. I didn't mean to upset him."

"Well, it's not like you know all of our buttons yet."

"Of course not." I slid him a sardonic side-eye. "Because we've only been working intensely together for how many months now?"

"I meant other kinds of buttons." When I didn't respond, deciding not to approach the subject mentally, let alone verbally, he went on, "Some insider baseball? A heartfelt apology goes a long way with Drake."

I eagerly accepted *that* part of things before waiting in silence for Drake to leave the bathroom. The whole time, I felt terrible. I certainly hadn't meant to be insensitive, especially after he'd been so kind to me. I ran over different ways to apologize to him.

Finally, he re-emerged.

"Drake?"

"Yes?"

"I'm sorry I offended you. It was the last thing I meant to do. Please accept my sincere apology."

His face softened, which made me feel worse and better in the same two seconds.

"I overreacted, Tolly. I have some issues with people doubting my sincerity, as you can see." A laugh warmed those chiseled features a little more. "I shouldn't have snapped at you like that. I hope *you* can forgive *me.*"

"Hey"—I patted the seat beside me—"let's call it even, okay?"

"Okay." He sat and buckled in for the landing.

Fletcher did the same on the other side, and we all watched out the windows as we dipped in over the mountains of the Las Vegas Valley. The landing strip at McCarran International appeared ahead.

"Perfect," Drake said as soon as we taxied to the private charters terminal. "The driver is already here. We've got work to do—and we need to get this little one something to eat." He unbuckled and stood the moment the pilot flashed the lights to tell him he could.

"Agreed." Fletcher was up and moving with the same

palpable impatience. "Something healthy. She usually likes something light in the afternoons."

It was my turn for exasperation. "Please stop talking about me like I'm not right here. And surprise, surprise, I can decide when and what I want to eat all on my own." I braced both hands to my waist. "What's gotten into the two of you? We've been working together for months. We left San Diego for Vegas, not Mars. A few hundred miles doesn't put you in charge of my well-being. And news flash number two—I've been away from home before."

Drake waited with forced patience, his expression plainly conveying the are-you-finished-yet? vibe, and then softly explained, "I thought low blood sugar might be contributing to your headache."

"I told you it was gone."

"And it would suck if it returned."

I squirmed, suddenly sheepish. If it was due to his obvious concern, his domineering tone, or both, I couldn't tell. "You're right. It would."

"We have a lot of work ahead of us tomorrow. The trade show's going to be insane. Besides, Fletch and I want to treat you to a celebration dinner afterward."

"If you'll allow us." Fletcher's interjection came with a pointed look at his friend. They'd clearly discussed this plan already, as well as my role in it. The knowledge brought on a thrill—and a shiver. "The hotel we're staying at, the Nyte, has some amazing chefs at their house restaurants."

"We're staying at the Nyte?" I didn't hide my astonishment. "I checked out their website when they announced the show would be there, but... Well, you two really travel in style, don't you?"

Fletcher shrugged. "It's where the show is taking place. Doesn't it make the most sense?"

"Sense or not, I'm going to have some explaining to do when I turn in my expense report. One night there will blow my entire month's allotment."

"SGC has taken care of everything," Drake assured. "They put us up in a suite, so I don't want to hear another word about expenses or costs for the rest of the weekend. Clear?"

He'd turned to address me while we waited for the plane to be secured, a move that trapped me tightly in the aisle between Fletcher and him. But that wasn't what started my stammering.

"A...s-suite? As in, we're all staying together? I-I'm not so sure that's a good idea, you guys."

"What's the problem, Tolly?" Fletcher's response vibrated into my hair. "There are two bedrooms and two bathrooms, separated by a living space. The suite's probably bigger than your whole apartment."

Drake nodded, never taking his eyes off me. One side of his wickedly full mouth kicked up. "I'm sure we won't get under each other's skin too badly for one weekend."

Before I could say anything, he pivoted back around, ducking to clear the doorway of the plane and pulling his sunglasses down from his head to shield his eyes from the desert sun. Could he look anything more like some flawless hunk from a fashion ad?

"Wait!" Only shock brought back my voice. I hurried after him, blurting as we descended the stairs to the tarmac, "How... how do you know..."

He laughed. "What are you talking about, sweet thing?"

"Stop calling me those kinds of nicknames."

Fletcher was right behind me—until we reached the Cadillac Escalade, when he jumped ahead and opened the door, despite the driver waiting right next to the vehicle. He was absolutely edible in his Wayfarers and with his dark-gold, wind-tossed hair. How had both of them managed to get better-looking since San Diego?

"Does *baby* suit you better?" he teased, motioning me into the car.

"No."

"Hop in," he directed. "It'll take just a few minutes to get all the bags off the plane. Honey?"

His teasing tone made me smile, even though I was trying to sound firm when I answered. "No way."

I slid into the Escalade. Of course this model had a bench seat in the back instead of captain's chairs. I was sure the men would sandwich me in as soon as they entered. I noticed their habit of capturing me between them whenever they had the opportunity. The realization made butterflies battle in my stomach like kamikaze pilots, especially as I spied on the two of them through the windshield.

So powerful. So commanding. So gorgeous. So perfect.

What the hell is going on here?

I needed to get a grip on myself and this situation before I did something really dumb. First step *had* to be insisting on my own room at the hotel—but I already knew I couldn't afford even a broom closet at the Nyte. It made even upscale places look like hobo shacks. With Cos Con in town, and on such short notice, I'd be lucky to get a room at a budget special down the street. In addition, SGC had made the travel arrangements. If they wanted our entire team rooming together, then we probably needed to stick with that plan.

I closed my eyes so I could stop tormenting myself with the sight of those two gods. As I leaned my head back, I tried to settle my thoughts down. My Jell-O limbs from the plane were definitely gone and forgotten.

Something had to be done, and quickly.

"Love." Drake slid in on my left, sinful grin playing at his lips while he spoke.

"Are you kidding me?"

"I like that one best." Fletcher folded his tall frame in on my right.

"It really rolls off the tongue." They bantered back and forth over the top of my head.

"Please stop," I snapped. "*Please* stop...all of this. I'm serious." I was freaking out and needed to let them see that. Their frowns told me I'd finally gotten through.

Drake cupped the back of my neck with a big, warm hand. "*Talia.* Settle down. We're playing around. As for the situation at the hotel, it's just a box in a building with places to sleep, not a marriage proposal. Let's just check in, take a look around, and if you're still worried, we'll make other arrangements. The last thing either of us would do is put you in a position you aren't comfortable with. Can you trust us on this?"

His touch worked its magic all over again, soothing my tension away in seconds. Fletcher added to the effect with his easy laugh.

"I'm pretty sure that when you see the place, you'll be fine with it. You won't even know we're there if you don't want to, angel."

Out came his killer smile again, and I couldn't help but smile back.

Damn it, these two were trouble.

Big, dangerous, sexy trouble.

ANGEL PAYNE & VICTORIA BLUE

CHAPTER SEVEN

The Nyte was just as magnificent as I'd heard.

"Wow," I whispered while the driver circled the Escalade into the glittering porte cochère and then hopped out to get our luggage.

He was assisted by a young man with boy-band hair and an equally dazzling grin, attracting the attention of at least six teenagers, a trio of cougars, and a couple of sugar daddies while performing his duties.

"Welcome to the Nyte, Mr. Newland and Mr. Ford," he greeted. "How was your flight in from San Diego?"

Drake nodded deferentially, as if they received this kind of reception at hotels all the time. "Excellent," he answered the youth. "Thank you, Tripp."

"Perfect," the kid answered. Eager as a puppy, he handed Fletcher an embossed business card. "I've already checked. Your suite is ready. I'll have the bags taken up right away. You have the number to text if you need the car again."

"Outstanding," Fletcher answered. He extended a tip and asked, "How are things going at UNLV?"

"Right on track to graduate," Tripp answered. "Then I'll be ready to move into Mr. Beckett's management program here."

Fletcher clapped him on the back. "Good job, man."

During the exchange, Drake tipped the driver and then leaned in to help me out of the car. The desert air hit me, dry and warm but hinting at the chill it would bring after sunset. The exotic flowers blooming in the planters added a touch of sexy spice to the balmy breeze—so *not* what I needed for thinking clearly at the moment. I had to focus on alternate lodging ideas. Just the thought of it was torture.

Instead, I took in my surroundings. The hotel was breathtaking. Gold and silver trimmed every surface, while crystal accents created tiny rainbows on every reflective plane. I'd read there were sixty floors in the hotel and secretly hoped our suite was nowhere near the top. Admitting my irrational fear of heights to these two would be mortifying. I already felt so small and insignificant in their presence.

At the front desk, another handsome young man greeted Fletcher by name. I couldn't help being impressed and proud that I was here with him. He was a force to be reckoned with, that was for sure, but was also greeted with affection and respect, in line with a reputation that he had clearly earned.

"Wesley. So nice to see you again." Fletcher shook the clerk's hand while motioning Drake and me closer. "You remember my very good friend, Drake Newland?"

"Indeed! Mr. Newland, it's wonderful to see you again. How are you?"

"I'm well, Wesley. Thank you for asking. May I also introduce our associate, Talia Perizkova? She'll be staying with us in the suite this weekend."

"Very good! Well, we are all at your service, Ms. Perizkova. Please make my staff or me aware if you require anything to make your stay more enjoyable. At the Nyte, we strive to transform your every desire into reality."

I didn't say a thing. Just stood and smiled like an idiot, wondering if adorable little Wesley *really* wanted to know my deepest desire at that moment—especially as Drake pressed his hand against the small of my back. His touch seared through the layers of my dress, making it impossible to think clearly. I blushed, instantly and profusely. Wesley didn't seem to notice—but ohhh, boy, did both the men at my sides.

"Everything's set with your account information." Wesley slid an elegant key packet across the marble counter. "Here are your keys and suite number. I understand Tripp and his team are already handling your bags. Again, welcome to the Nyte."

We headed from the lobby, through the casino, and toward the elevator bank to find our suite. The elevator was full of other guests, stopping at least three times before we picked up speed and soared higher and higher. My stomach rolled as I watched the numbers quietly dinging. Finally, the doors slid open...

At the fifty-third floor.

Drake held the lift's exit open, and as soon as I realized the outside wall was dominated by huge glass panes, I grabbed Fletcher's hand. So much for keeping my little secret any longer—though, with Fletcher returning my grip, silently assuring my safety through the strength of his fingers, I was able to get in a centering breath and admire the luxury as we entered.

The hotel's décor was stunning, even here. My heels sank into plush gold carpeting, and all the sconces on the walls were made of crystal. The windows were also framed in gold, as if the view itself were a work of art. I couldn't argue. Once the sun went down, the view of the Strip would be amazing.

I let Fletcher lead the way to the end of the hall, where one door stood alone, taller than the others we had passed. Drake swiped the key card over the reader on the wall. He pushed open the door and stepped sideways, letting Fletcher guide me inside the suite. I had to hide a smile while an image flared to mind, as shocking as it was fleeting. I actually pictured Fletcher carrying me over the threshold as Drake looked on, glowing with love and pride.

Whoa, baby.

Sheez. Wherever that had come from, it needed to return right now, to its rightful place—wherever the hell *that* was. I was here to do my job, not get lost in the fantasy seeming to unravel from me faster by the minute.

Or maybe it was me who was unraveling?

"You don't like it?"

Fletcher's voice, sounding so let down, jerked me back to reality.

"Huh?" I snapped my head up.

He was staring at me with the same intensity as Drake, watching as if I were damn near prey, gauging every nuance of my reaction.

"I asked if you liked it."

Drake stepped over. "Tolly...you look like you've seen a ghost. What's up?"

Crap. Where was a quick comeback when a girl needed one? I couldn't possibly tell them about my—what *had* that been? A fantasy? A yearning?

A freaking pipe dream?

"No. I love it!"

Drake shifted closer. Even closer. There I was, standing in the gilded foyer of the most incredible hotel suite I'd ever seen, toe-to-toe with an even more splendorous sight—Drake Newland's carved, perfect, archangel face.

With one finger under my chin, he brought my gaze up to

his. "But what?"

I gulped. He already knew I was lying. The set of his eyes, so dark and determined, said as much.

"There...there is no but. I was just...I was thinking—"

"Spit it out, girl." Fletcher backtracked in order to crowd in behind me.

No tight private plane spacing this time—just him deliberately pressing close...and sending shivers down to the ends of my toes.

"All right, all right." Just move away. Just stay. Oh God, what am I doing here? "I'm...afraid of heights."

Darn it! I hadn't wanted to spill it, but right now, it was the safer of two truths. Like I could even consider the alternative. *So I just had this vision as we walked over the threshold... You guys are never going to believe this...*

And they wouldn't.

No matter how anything turned out over this weekend, conjugal bliss was far, *far* from the equation.

"What does that have to do with anything?" Drake was gentle but firm about it, adding a second finger in order to hold me in place.

"Excuse me?" I was glad for the tiny surge of ire, helping me step from his numbing grasp. I paced deeper into the suite, motioning around the room with a small twirl. "You can see all these windows too, right? This view must include even the Hoover Dam, I'm sure of it." I dropped my arms while backing away from the big window. "But you can also see all the way down to the street. And yeah, that scares me...a little."

"Not an issue." Fletcher shrugged. "We'll just get a room on a lower floor."

He made it all sound so simple. I just wondered why I

wasn't convinced.

"But we'll have to warn you, sweet girl, the hotel doesn't have many suites below this level. If we move to a lower floor, we'll likely be sharing one room." Drake watched me with careful eyes.

Fletcher dropped the bomb. "And one bed."

I snapped a stare to where he stood, hands in pockets, grinning smugly. Damn it, he already knew we'd be staying in this suite. I could barely keep my cool with these two in a palace of a room like this, let alone something more...intimate.

"Okay, so this is fine. Yep, just fine. I mean, look around! It's more than fine—it's amazing. I'm just going to stay back from the windows, and everything will be fine, fine, fine. See? I'm better already. It's fine."

Drake dropped his head. Fletcher wasn't so subtle about his gloating chuckle. "So, do you always babble when you're nervous?"

"I'm not nervous."

His hands came up, palms out. "Whatever you say, sugar."

"Stop that. And I'm *not* nervous. *Why* would I be nervous?"

"Right. Got that. Everything's—what was the word, bro?"

"Fine." Drake's single syllable shook with laughter.

"Exactly," I snapped. "It's *fine*. This is just the three of us, making it all fine, in a lovely and gigantic room. I'm going to take the bedroom on the right, if the two of you are good with that?"

"Yep." Fletcher smirked. "That's just—"

"A dead horse now." I pivoted and marched toward the bedroom. "Can you put my bag by the door when it gets up here? I'm going to go freshen up a bit."

Not a minute too soon, I reached the bedroom and almost

slammed the door behind me. As I leaned against it, my heart thudded in my ears like a hunted animal's.

That had been a close call. Too close. My stupid daydreams. I couldn't entertain *any* more like that around these two. Between the pair, they didn't miss a single detail about what I said or how I acted.

This was going to be the longest weekend of my life.

Or the best weekend of my life.

A soft tap came from the other side of the door. I jumped out of my deep thoughts and wondered how long I had actually been standing there. Minutes? An hour?

"Sweetie, your bag is right outside here. Can I get you something from the bar?"

I answered back, almost too quickly. "You guys are leaving?"

Fletcher's chuckle was warm and enticing, even through the barrier. Against my better instincts, I opened the door.

He greeted me with a smile. "We have a full bar out here in the sitting room." Gracefully, he extended a hand. God, he even had gorgeous hands. "Come join us. I promise we'll keep you far away from the windows."

While I hesitated, the devil returned to his smirk. The look was rapidly becoming my favorite, and I think he knew it. His eyes began twinkling too, but his mouth curled up more, a continued promise of delightful, sinful things.

Which meant I *really* needed to reject his offer.

"Okay." Damn it. I was so lost. The pitiful thing? I was pretty sure he knew that, as well.

He reveled in what he was doing to me, though his touch was respectful as he gently reached out and twined my hand against his.

Walking down the small hallway leading back to the suite's main space, he looked down to where our hands were entangled. "Is this all right?"

Annnnd, melting of bones officially commenced. Now he was asking permission? It was so Southern and boyish... and so different from the bossy, never-take-no-as-an-answer approach of Drake. I couldn't decide which enticed me more— or if I even wanted to decide. Maybe it explained why they always bedded women together. The combo had something to please any and every woman. They would never miss with this angle. Well, *angles.*

I couldn't really coax sound out of my throat, so I just nodded.

Fletcher smiled again. "Good. I rather like touching you."

He said it so quietly, I almost couldn't make out the whole sentence. I envisioned pulling on his collar to make him come back and repeat it.

Oh, God. Me and my runaway fantasies. *Again.*

In the living room, Drake was behind the bar, seeming very much at home. But of course, he was an expert at artisan cocktails too. Both of these men seemed to master everything they took on.

"What can I fix you, beautiful?"

I leaned against the dark-wood counter. "Can you make a margarita? On the rocks, please?"

With one deft move, he yanked down a rocks glass from the shelf. "Can I make a margarita, she asks!" He shared a hearty chuckle with Fletch before drawling, "Sweet girl, you are looking at a mix master. And my personal favorite poison?"

I slid a smile out. "Tequila?"

Fletcher waggled his eyebrows. "Such a quick study."

I held up both hands. "Well, take it easy on me. We still have a lot of work to get through today, and then there's all day tomorrow. The last thing I need is a hangover."

Fletcher nodded. "Not to worry. We'll have one drink and then go downstairs and check out the booth setup in the meeting hall. I want to make sure the positioning is exactly what we specified and confirm all the power got dropped to the right spots too."

I expanded my smile. When we talked business like this, the three-way flow was easy, even energetic. If I could only keep steering things in that direction...

Like a margarita in my hand was going to help.

Nevertheless, I accepted the drink from Drake and raised my glass to them both. "To the three of us and success!" After they echoed the words and we all sipped—perhaps I did a little more than sip, because Drake really did concoct an amazing margarita—I went on. "Tomorrow is the start of a much-needed new beginning for me—in more ways than you can imagine." Considering all the kindness they'd shown me today alone caused tears to prick to the backs of my eyes. "I'm so thankful I was partnered with the two of you."

God. Had I said too much?

"Hear, hear!"

We all clinked glasses, but I noticed I was the only one taking a second sip. Both men were staring at me with utterly unreadable expressions. Uh-oh, maybe I *had* said too much.

"Hey. No fair. Why aren't you drinking?"

Fletcher ran a finger around the rim of his copper mug. "Just taking it all in. Taking *you* in. I could watch you for hours, Tolly."

"I'll beat you to it." Drake looked wistful with his

admission. *Wistful?* Ohhh yeah. Wistful.

Oh, man, this was weird. And wonderful. But mostly weird. No...mostly wonderful. I had no idea anymore.

"Would you two stop?" I gestured angrily at their drinks in hand. "Seriously! Drink your beers—and whatever that thing is—so we can go downstairs." I really didn't have any idea about how else to react to their declarations, so I went for the irked ostrich approach. I jammed my head in the proverbial sand and kept pretending our dynamic wasn't changing so drastically.

"It's a Moscow Mule," Fletch offered, finally taking a sip of his drink.

"A what?" It had been a while since I'd gone clubbing or to a bar, so I wasn't familiar with the drink at all.

"A Moscow Mule. I've become deeply interested in Russian particulars recently." His smug smile didn't go unnoticed, although I tried to play it off like I didn't pick up on his innuendo.

I pointed at my glass, now half drained. How had *that* happened? "Whatever you say. I'm going to stick to the old standby. But I really like the pretty copper cup."

"Only you would appreciate the cup and not the drink inside." His words, still quiet, were joined by teasing lights in his eyes, dancing over the mug's rim as he took another taste.

"Who said I didn't appreciate the drink? I've never even tried one."

"Well, then. Let's remedy that."

He stepped closer to me, the mug still clutched in his hand. Something about him, an energy I didn't dare deny, forced my gaze up to his face. I couldn't tear my eyes from him when he slowly raised his drink to my lips. Out of instinct, I put my hand on top of his, though I let him tilt the cup until ice-cold liquor wet my tongue. A riot of tastes bombarded me. Ginger and lime and vodka, tangling in a mix of smooth and zesty, making my nose tickle and my blood warm.

The drink...was just like him. A thousand different things blended beneath one sleek copper and gold package.

More, please.

I watched his pupils dilate as I let the sip slide in and then started to pull away. Despite my thirst, for the drink *and* the man, I'd had enough.

Our hands lowered the cup back down, but our gazes never parted. In a brazen move, I dipped my tongue out to taste the sweetness left behind on my lips. Fletcher's eyes grew wider—just before a sharp inhalation broke our woven spell. We both turned to see Drake watching us with fascination. His mouth was partly open, his stare enraptured...probably a mirror image of my own.

"That was fantastic," he rasped.

Fletcher echoed the low snarl. "You read my mind. I had a few other words in there, but yeah—fantastic."

Warning bells sounded in my subconscious. Ohhhh, man. We were dancing, and not in a good way. Or maybe jumping. Back and forth. Appropriate. Inappropriate. Appropriate. Waaaay inappropriate.

"Is it warm in here?" Drake, clearly trying to lighten the sensual aftermath, stepped from behind the bar and stalked to the climate-control pad on the wall.

As he adjusted the temperature down by a few degrees, I investigated the rest of the suite. There was a small kitchenette with a breakfast bar and a sitting area with the wet bar and small conference table, as well as a beautiful sectional sofa facing a fireplace and a huge, wall-mounted monitor. The suite's two bedrooms were off to each side.

"Hey, guys?" I pivoted back toward them. "If I'm in the one room and there's only one other room left, does one of you have to sleep on the couch?"

They shrugged in unison. I instantly saw they hadn't given it a moment's thought.

"Ohhh no. That's not going to work. At all. I should take the sofa and you guys should take the rooms. I'll move my bag out into the foyer."

Drake blocked my beeline back to the room containing my things. "You will do no such thing."

"The heck I won't. It's not fair, Drake. Your expense account is taking the hit for this palace. *I'm* the third wheel. *I'll* take the sofa."

"Talia."

Crap. There was that tone again. How did he manage to freeze my thoughts by just intoning my name? It was starting to tick me off. I wasn't some child getting into mischief. This was something altogether different.

But damn it, if I didn't just stand there, staring at him with wide eyes.

"I've done two tours in the Middle East. I've slept on dirt, sand, and steel. Sleeping on a plush sofa isn't going to be a hardship. Now, no more arguing."

He didn't wait for a retort. Just headed back over to the bar and finished his beer in silence.

Okay, then.

Stewing a little, I plopped down on the sofa with my margarita and rested my head back on the low cushions. He was probably right. This thing would be great to sleep on. I was totally talking myself down so it didn't feel as though I had just been chastised like an errant teenager. The independent woman I was fighting so hard to be roared at me to go stand up for myself and push the issue. But the tired, overworked girl said just let it go. I finished the rest of my drink in one gulp.

"Ready when you are." I smoothed my dress as I waited for the guys to grab their wallets.

"Let's go see what we can find out."

Drake and Fletch each put a key card in their wallet. When I stretched out a hand for my own and was met with a pair of blank stares, my expression turned into a glare.

"Tolly?" Drake arched both eyebrows. "Problem?"

"A key?" I prompted. "For me?"

"Oh, they only gave us two."

"Excuse me?"

Fletcher winked. "Now you can't wander off."

"Really? Because I seem like the wandering type?"

Drake's brow furrowed. "She has a point."

"Yeah. She does."

I openly fumed. "*She* is also *still* here."

"Another good point." Fletcher tucked his wallet into his jacket. "But...you never know. You may just get tired of our asses and want to go off on your own."

"Again...really?"

"Oh!" A lightbulb practically appeared in the air over his head. "I hear they have an amazing spa here too. Maybe we should check that out while we're downstairs. Schedule some services for the day after the show?"

"Great idea, brother. Since we have the jet and don't have to worry about making a flight, we can stay all day. We could even spend the night again, if things go well—at the trade show." He added the last of it as if Fletcher had kicked him from under an invisible table.

"I don't know." Unbelievably, I still sounded like the wet blanket. "I just can't ever justify spending that kind of money for nothing."

"Nothing?" Drake rebutted. "When was the last time you had a full-body massage? I'm not sure I *wouldn't* pay money for that. Or a facial? Or you could get your nails done...or whatever shit women do." He waved a hand in the air to encompass the shit he was referring to.

It pulled a little laugh out of me. He had so many adorable behaviors hidden under his tough exterior.

"Still seems like a waste of hard-earned money to me," I persisted. "I can paint my own nails."

I came from a large family, where money was a constant topic at the dinner table. Or should I say the lack of it, as in making what we had stretch for everyone. Massages? Pedicures? They weren't part of my reality then, nor were they now.

The elevator ride was quiet. The guys both seemed wrapped up in their own thoughts. I wasn't much for chatter, so I busied my attention with the hotel's digital reader boards, discreet reminders of everything happening at the Nyte. The list was long, but a good portion of it was dedicated to events in conjunction with Cos Con. When those appeared, a thrill raced through my system. We'd worked so hard for this event, so I savored the excitement.

Once we were back on the ground floor—the only level that made sense in my book—Drake led the charge through the throng of guests and casino players. Fletcher was his wingman but held my hand tightly, as he had in our suite. The action never even crossed my mind as being inappropriate until we got to the conference center entrance and were back among our industry peers.

As soon as I pulled my hand back, Fletcher's stare sharpened. "What?"

"*What*, what?"

And yet more sharpness, the azure glints of his stunning eyes turning cool. "Why'd you pull away?"

I jabbed up my chin. This wasn't like the dispute about the couch. We were back to real life now. Back to the shit that really mattered about this weekend. "I just don't think this is the place. People will misunderstand."

"Will they?"

"Why do you answer everything with another question? It's infuriating."

"There's something I'd like to see." His eyes glimmered with heated thoughts.

"What's that?" Drake finally realized we were no longer right behind him and doubled back.

"Our little one," Fletch clarified, "all fired up."

"First of all, I'm not anyone's 'little one.' Second, you *really* don't want to see the whole 'fired up' thing. I'm serious. You need to get that through your skulls, okay?" *Your really gorgeous, very...* "You guys just don't understand what it's like for a woman in the business world." I lowered my voice so only they could hear me. "If people think we are together in any other way than we actually are, as business associates, all of the hard work I've done will be for nothing."

"I can sense you're serious about this, but I'm sorry, I still don't get what you're talking about."

Fletcher took a step closer, trying to comfort me with his

presence, but it had the opposite effect this time. I stamped a foot back and launched a mini tirade.

"You know damn well how people whisper about the girl in the office who slept her way to the top. I refuse to be that girl. I've worked so hard on this project for the past few months. Way too hard to have it all thrown away because a rumor started spreading that I didn't earn whatever success we may have coming."

I imagined myself stepping down off a soapbox and it poofing into thin air. A crazy giggle erupted from my throat, making both of the guys look at me like I was losing it.

"Okay, okay. I see where you're coming from, and I apologize for making you uncomfortable. I won't slip again."

"It's not like that..." The thought of either one of them no longer flirting or sneaking in little touches here and there instantly made me sad.

Fletcher cocked his head to the side, trying to read me, while Drake just seemed frustrated.

"I'm so confused right now."

"It's cool, D. I'll explain in man-speak later. Let's check in at the registration table and find out where they put us."

While Fletcher spoke with the attendant at the desk, Drake grabbed a map showing the booth layout for the event, and I picked up our ID badges.

"Looks like we are in booth twenty-five in the 'On the Rise' section. I don't think I like that they have all of the new product lines in one spot. They should've put us throughout the hall."

"I agree. I guess if we ever run a trade show, we can do it better. In the meantime, twenty-five it is. According to the map, we're just inside the east entrance to the hall. That makes up for the 'lumping us all together' mistake, I think. We'll either be the first thing people see when they come in or the last thing as they leave. I like it." I lowered the map to find both Drake and Fletch just staring at me, grinning with approval.

"What?" Suddenly I felt self-conscious.

"Just appreciating your brilliance."

I rolled my eyes and headed toward the east entrance of the hall. I could hear the guys talking to each other right behind me, so I knew they were in tow. The booth was just what we'd hoped for. The size was perfect, and I really was pleased with the location. Drake checked to ensure we had electrical power routed to the area, and we did a quick run-through of the display.

When we'd finished in the exhibit hall, we wound our way back through the casino to the spa. The men insisted we all schedule massages for the day after the show, knowing that standing on a concrete floor all day would take a toll on our bodies. My lower back was already hurting at the thought of it.

Back out in the casino, we wandered by a few banks of slot machines.

"Let's test Lady Luck; what do you say?" Fletcher parked himself on the stool in front of the machine. *Lucky 7* was in red, white, and blue across the top, and the promise of jackpot payouts lit up all around.

"How much is this per try?" I was never one for gambling— again, wasting money on skewed chance games just didn't strike me as prudent.

Drake explained to me how you could play just one dollar or up to three on each pull. Fletcher fed the machine a twenty and gave the big handle on the side a dramatic pull.

"I should've rubbed you for luck first," he said with a

mischievous grin.

The reels came to a halt, and just like that, three dollars were gone. He repeated the process but before pulling the handle stroked my hair for luck. Again—nothing.

"So much for me being a lucky charm."

We stood by and watched him lose twenty hard-earned dollars within five minutes. I just shook my head, thinking, *Better him than me.* What was crazy, though, was the number of people within eyesight doing the exact same thing—pumping machines full of their hard-to-come-by cash in hopes of a bigger dream. I was amazed and confused about what, exactly, I was missing.

"See, once you win, you want to keep going. You hope for the chance that you might hit it again. It becomes addictive pretty quickly." Drake easily rested his hand on my lower back as we strolled and he tried to explain the fascination with gambling to me.

"Maybe you would like twenty-one more. Or maybe roulette?"

"I can't see the appeal of losing money, no matter how it happens. I just don't think gambling is for me."

"Fair enough. Do you want to get something to eat? Or look through the shops while we're down here?"

"I'd really like to go to the room and prepare for tomorrow. I want to run over some key talking points a few times and maybe lose myself in that enormous tub I have in my bathroom. Do you have that on your side too?"

"You know what they say, Tolly. All work and no play—"

"Give her a break, Fletch. If she doesn't want to gamble, then so be it. It's not for everyone."

"Okay, okay. Let's head up to the room and we can order

room service."

"If you guys want to stay down here and play some more, I can go up to the room myself. I am an adult, after all." I gave them a little smile, letting them know I wasn't being ungrateful that they wanted to see to my every need but that they should do what they wanted too.

"That's a decent idea, actually. Dude, let's play a little roulette and then head up for dinner in the suite. Here, Tolly, take my key card, and we'll see you in a bit, okay?"

Drake was looking at his best friend like he'd just sprouted another head. Clearly he wasn't on board with the plan, but he could tell Fletcher had something on his mind. He leaned in to me and very slowly gave me a whisper of a kiss on my cheek. He smelled so good standing so close to me, I wanted to grab on to his thick biceps and hold him in place for a few more seconds.

Not to be outdone, after I took the key card from Fletcher, he repeated the process, but on my other cheek. One soft, easy, butterfly kiss ignited my bloodstream like a branding iron instead. I swayed on my feet after he stepped away, already missing them both as they turned and walked deeper into the crowd of people.

I spun on my heel and headed to the elevators. Luckily, a car stood with its doors open, and I was able to quickly escape to gather myself. What just happened back there? Of course they had been sneaking in little touches here and there, a brush of my hair off my shoulder while I'd spoken, the brief hand holding, standing so close I had felt their heat. But those had been *kisses*. Two of them to be exact. And my cheeks still burned where their lips had touched my skin. This train barreling down the tracks was about to be derailed. If I didn't put my foot down soon, trouble would follow. Every little step over the line was going to add up to one gigantic mistake.

So why were my panties wet?

A flush spread across my face again at the realization of how turned on I was. Maybe I needed a cold shower instead of a warm, soothing bath.

I reached our suite and slid the key card across the reader. With a small green light and a click of the lock, I was safely back inside and blissfully alone.

I ran a bath in the small-pool-sized tub. I took advantage of the products on the ledge and added some lavender bath salts to the flowing water. The amazing, calming scent filled the room in pillows of steam. It felt so good to get out of the clothes I'd been wearing all day as I left everything in a heap on the floor where I'd undressed.

So unlike me. But this whole trip so far was so unlike me. From the massages on the plane, to standing up for myself in the convention hall, only to be swept away again by two innocent kisses on my cheek.

They just hadn't felt that innocent. My thoughts at the moment certainly weren't innocent either. While I soaked in the tub, I could still smell their colognes, feel their body heat, imagine what their touches would feel like on my body. I hadn't been with a man since the disaster called Gavin, and my body had grown lonely. And needy.

I floated in the tub and let myriad fantasies run through my mind. What would it be like to be with two men at one time? Before meeting Drake and Fletcher, I hadn't given it a moment's thought, but suddenly it was something I wanted to discover for myself. If only they weren't the men I worked with. That in itself put the whole scenario back into focus. What on earth was I thinking? The reality of the situation came crashing in unwelcomed. We could not keep crossing well-defined professional lines. My career was the most important thing in my life at the moment, and I was on the precipice of a huge leap forward. If the launch went well tomorrow, the sky would be the limit for me. I needed to keep my head in the game and my libido out of it. I just needed to get through dinner with them, and then I would excuse myself and stay locked in my room for the rest of the night so I wouldn't be tempted any more.

With a mental game plan in place, I lifted the drain with my toes and hopped in the shower to rinse off and wash my hair. I grabbed the fluffiest robe I had ever seen off the hook on the back of the door and wrapped myself in it like a baby. I combed out my long, dark hair and twisted it up into a makeshift bun on top of my head, tucking the ends in so it would stay in place.

I lay back on the bed, sinking into the down duvet and perfect pillows. Hotels always had the best pillows. My eyes grew so heavy I just couldn't fight it anymore. I drifted off contently for a nap, floating in a sea of goose down and cotton.

I had left the door to my bedroom open when I'd fallen asleep, so the sound of deep voices shook me awake. The sun had gone down outside, leaving the suite dim and peaceful. I didn't want to wake up—my body felt like a lead weight, so calm and serene in that glorious bed. I knew I should get up, but I lay there with my eyes closed, listening to the men out in the living room.

"She's sleeping like a goddess, all fuckable and amazing in nothing but a robe. It looks like every fantasy I've ever had of her."

Drake must have come to my door and gone back again to report his findings. A smile played on my lips. *He thinks I'm a goddess? That I look fuckable?*

Warning! Keeping it professional. Right.

Those things shouldn't have made me happy to overhear. They should have made me bound to my feet and set the men straight about our relationship.

"I think she was freaking out earlier though. I could see it in her eyes. When you surprised the hell out of both of us with that kiss in the casino, she looked dizzy with lust and then immediately at war with herself about it. I figured if I followed it up quickly with more positive, she would see it was what she wanted too."

"Yeah, I can tell we'll have to go ever so slowly with her or she'll spook on us. She's like a little fawn out on its own for the first time. The innocence in her mannerisms—makes my dick hard enough to pound nails."

"That's really poetic, man."

Fletcher's laugh at his own joke filled the suite, making me smile again, even while I was processing what they'd said. They were definitely putting the moves on me. It wasn't my lonely imagination. Now, to figure out a way to make them stop.

Even though that was the last thing I wanted.

ANGEL PAYNE & VICTORIA BLUE

CHAPTER EIGHT

Drake hung up the phone as I padded into the living area
of our suite. Having overheard the feedback from him and
Fletcher about the robe, I'd decided to pull on some joggers
and a loose tank top rather than flitting around in the garment
that was already inspiring them to wickedness again. Best to
defuse the situation now, with something more appropriate.

"Hey, Sleeping Beauty." Fletcher sat next to me on the
sofa. "We just ordered some dinner. They said it should be
about thirty minutes. Are you hungry?"

"Starving, now that you mention it." I rose. "I'd better call
down and get something too. After we eat, we can run through
talking points for tomorrow."

Drake approached, looking a little pissed. Maybe a lot.
Unwittingly, I shivered—and obeyed at once when he motioned
for me to sit again.

"Do you seriously think we'd order for ourselves and not
get anything for you?"

Yikes. I didn't really know how to handle him. "Well, uh...I
don't know. I—how—well, what did you order? How would you
even know what I like and don't like?"

"Talia."

Damn. *Oh please, not the voice.* It shot straight to the V
between my legs—in every perfect way possible. How twisted
was I that a man so daunting could also make me so hot?

"Drake." It came out on a whisper, a lover's caress—even

though I was meant to be standing up for myself.

"We've been together for months, day and night, putting this project together. I could probably catalog what you've eaten, how many times you've ordered certain things, and your exact reaction each time you've lifted a fork to your mouth."

The facial expression warned me he was deadly serious. Any hope of breaking the strange tension with a nutritionally obsessed joke was lost.

"Ohhhkaayy." It truly was the best answer I could come up with.

"How about this? If you don't absolutely love what I've ordered for you, I'll repay the debt with a massage." He wiggled his fingers in the air. "You know all about the magic in these bad boys."

I laughed. I couldn't help it. His silly side was so endearing—and fascinating. He could shift from one mood to another like no one I'd known before. It was a little unsettling too.

"That's a pretty bold offer, mister. I may pretend to not like my food just so you'll have to pay up."

He arched one dark eyebrow. "Do you think you could lie to either one of us and get away with it? We would know the second it came off your tongue. You're a terrible liar, Talia Perizkova, and we all know it."

It was true. I couldn't lie to save my own life. Even as a child, I'd gotten into so much trouble by ratting myself out, unable to take the pressure of having to weave a plausible story. In response to his insight, all I could offer was a dorky grin. In return, Drake and Fletch watched me with their hawk eyes. *Thanks for nothing, guys.* Somehow, over the past few months, these two stunningly gorgeous men had learned my every fault and feature—and now all I could do was act like a blithering idiot in front of them.

"Let's change the subject," I suggested eagerly, nodding at Drake. "Maybe you could make me one of those amazing margaritas again. I suddenly feel like a good stiff drink."

I swore Drake mumbled something about "other stiff things" as he stomped back to the bar. Fletcher's bark of a laugh confirmed I wasn't hearing things.

Keep it professional, damn it. Danger, Will Robinson!

Once Drake brought my drink, we all sat together and threw around a few ideas about the show the next morning. We'd have a mixture of independent and big box buyers at the booth. Everyone needed an individualized approach. I sipped on the tasty cocktail, which helped with the energy of the conversation. These exchanges always invigorated me. While both these men possessed brilliant business minds, they considered every single one of my ideas on equal footing with their own. Everything was so much easier with them when we could restrict the subject to work. This was where the conversation needed—*needed*—to stay.

There was a knock on the door, and we all surged to our feet, but I stopped the guys with a raised hand.

"At least let me answer the door. All of your waiting on me is really going to my head." I rolled my eyes to let them know I was only half joking. "What will I do when we get home and no one is there to jump at my smallest whim?"

"We could fix that too."

I wasn't sure who said that to my retreating back when I rushed to let in the staff with our food. Everything smelled amazing, like luxury spun into edible form, before the waiter from room service had even lifted the silver domes from the plates. But when he did, all the savory aromas had my mouth watering. All of my favorites were spread before me—shrimp cocktail to start, an amazing rib-eye for dinner, and warm apple cobbler for dessert.

Well...wow. They really did have me pegged.

Drake and Fletcher joined me at the table as we dug into the most amazing room service meal I'd ever scarfed. And yes, scarfed was the proper verb. After just my first bite, I could barely look up from my plate. It felt like I hadn't eaten in days.

"You win." I finally took a break to concede it, pushing away the entrée plate I'd all but slurped clean. Drake threw out a cocky chuckle as I pointed my fork at the other plate, still filled with the cobbler. "This is amazing. You really did pick all my favorites. I don't even remember ever having dessert with you guys. How did you know?"

Drake's laugh mellowed to a knowing look. "One day, I heard you talking to your mother on the phone. You were making apologies—*not* easy ones—about being disappointed you couldn't be with the family for Sunday dinner, favorite desert included, due to a deadline we had. However she replied left you pretty ruined before you sucked it up and plastered the game face back on." He swung his head to Fletcher, who nodded that he'd witnessed the exact same moment. "We both felt terrible, knowing you were missing time with your family so you could stay and work on the launch. Then and there, we agreed to make it up to you eventually."

For a long moment, I just stared at him. Then Fletch. Drake again. That had to be the most thoughtful thing anyone had done for me in a long damn time. When I'd been with Gavin, everything had been about—well, Gavin. Only now did I fully realize how selfish and self-absorbed he'd really been.

Gavin March probably wouldn't have known if I loved shrimp or was allergic to them, let alone ordered the exact cut of steak I preferred, cooked so that it melted on my tongue with each and every bite.

I blinked through vision that had suddenly gone cloudy. The tears thickened, threatening to fall at any moment. Trying to hold them back just made it worse. Oh, God. Talk about embarrassment.

"Whoa." Drake shot up, circled the table, and filled the chair next to mine. "Tolly. Honey. What is it?"

I stopped him with a panicked hand on his arm. "No. *No.* Everything is perfect. It's just... It's just that I don't... I don't know how to say all of what I'm thinking...and feeling...and not sound like a sappy girl."

Fletcher came close on the other side by scooting his chair over. "We like sappy girls, baby. Can't you see that yet?"

"No one has ever done something like this. *All* of this." I dared glancing up at them both. "You notice things about me without being told outright. It's all...surreal."

His eyes darkened to cobalt. "You deserve to be taken care of."

I stiffened. "I can take care of myself."

"Okay, *listen* to what I just said. You *deserve* to be taken care of, not you *need* to be taken care of. It's a gift for us to do this. A privilege. You should be treated this way every single day, simply because of your kindness, your beauty...because you're you. It makes us happy to make you happy."

If he was trying to make things less surreal, he was failing.

I shifted in my seat and let him see every inch of my skeptical pout. "Well, from my experience, people 'just do nice things for others' so they can get what they want."

Fletcher leaned in a little more. With one hand on the table and one clasping the back of my chair, he was close enough that I got a deep inhalation of his obscenely masculine cologne, probably blended with the pheromones of a real stallion.

"Then you've been hanging around the wrong people, love."

His last word guaranteed I was now declaring more comments off-limits. Instead I busied myself with the cobbler. Outside of Mama's, this was the best version of the dessert I'd ever tasted. I closed my eyes, savoring all the amazing flavors playing hopscotch in my mouth.

Inside those three seconds, a warm hand covered mine.

I popped my eyes open to find Fletcher filling my view. He was just inches from my face, with a hungry look that made me squirm even more.

"Can I have a bite?" He barely whispered the request but moved his hand to let me lift the spoon.

Boldness took over. I dipped in the spoon, loading it with a generous bite before lifting it to his outrageously full lips. I watched his every move, holding my breath...hoping like hell not to break the spell.

His lips closed around the magical mush of dough, fruit, and sugar. He never ceased staring, as though boring right through my center, lighting me up from the inside like a Halloween pumpkin. Not breathing, I watched him chew slowly, seductively...entrancing me more deeply each second. And I let him. And ohhh, it felt good. So good.

When a bit of apple clung to his lips, I went ahead and obeyed all the new instincts flowing through me, swiping my finger at them. With an approving rumble, Fletcher grabbed my hand. He pulled my fingertip in, gently sucking, still keeping me prisoner to his deep-blue stare. I dragged in air, struggling to stay upright as my head swam with dizzy temptation...

But the moment my lips parted, he swooped in. His strong mouth pressed against mine, and I was completely lost, swept out to sea, consumed by the perfect current pounding between us. At that moment, I knew I had a choice, though it sure didn't feel like one. Larger forces than me—than even him—had been awakened. Though it was probably the most inappropriate thing I could do, I returned the kiss with all the strength in my body.

And I didn't want to stop.

Next to us, Drake had become a statue. It surprised me but turned me way the hell on. I felt him there, knowing he was watching every detail of Fletcher's mouth on mine. When he let out a rough hiss of approval, my desire was amped into the stratosphere. I was lost to any coherent thought and could only focus on the electricity jolting from where Fletcher toyed with my lips. He grew the intensity of the contact, pressing at my mouth with his incessant tongue, continuing to play along the seam where we meshed.

I could no longer fight him—or all the incredible things he made me feel. With a sigh, I willingly opened for his exploration. He tasted like cinnamon and warm brown sugar, making the kiss even sweeter than it would be naturally. I was victim to it all. I wanted it all. I tilted my head just a bit, making the fit even better. That caused a low groan from Drake, communicating what sounded like physical agony. What did that mean? Did he want to keep looking on...or was everything Margaux had told me about them really true? Did Drake want to...be a part of this?

I opened my eyes and pulled back from Fletcher, though I was unsure what to do next. What would happen next.

"That was so fucking hot. I've been dreaming about it for so long." Fletcher's eyes were heavy with desire.

With a jolt, I realized that I had been too. Kissing him had come so easily...so naturally.

And yeah...I wanted to kiss Drake too.

What on earth was happening to me?

And did I really want that answer right now?

I swiveled my gaze to Drake, summoning the sexiest look I could muster. "Do you...want a taste too?" *In for a penny...*

He nodded with slow, silent deliberation. I didn't miss the way his nostrils flared slightly, like a wild animal taking in his prey through all of his senses. It made my stomach dance, just as untamed, racing with excitement. That should have been my warning sign, my body's scream to stop, but I couldn't. I no longer wanted to.

Drake's kiss was completely different. He reached to the back of my skull, cradling my nape, dragging me closer until I tumbled from my chair into his, where I instantly felt his stiff cock straining through his pants. His lips met mine with force, making it nearly impossible to hold on to sanity. His tongue swept through my mouth, tasting, claiming, dominating. I sucked air in through my nose, his overwhelming presence making me swirl with dizziness. A whimper erupted in my throat, but I had no idea what it meant. How I felt. What I wanted.

Did I want them to stop?

Or did I long to barrel forward and never look back?

"Do you like the way Drake kisses you, baby? The way he holds you in place, bending you to his will?"

I came up for air long enough to hear Fletcher's taunting questions. Was he serious, though? Did he really expect me to answer such an obvious inquiry? Now? And why did it make every inch of my sex twist with new desire?

"I'm going to take that dreamy look in your eye as a yes." He chuckled a bit and moved in closer to Drake and me.

I didn't miss how Drake kept watching me, taking in every muscle tic, every inhaled breath. He was so sexy and powerful, his strong arm wrapped around my waist, the other hand still buried in my hair. He rubbed a thumb along my skull, massaging away any anxiety that developed when my head won the battle and ran away on a path of self-doubt.

"You are so beautiful," he finally whispered, his damp breath tickling my earlobe. He trailed a few kisses down my neck while tilting my head back for his own access.

Fletcher hummed out a deep approval. "You could say it fifty times a day, my brother, and it wouldn't be enough." He caressed down the other side of my neck. "Sweet girl, you are everything we dreamed you would be."

When I finally found the strength to speak, my voice was husky and low. "You've dreamed of me?"

"Every time I close my eyes," he drawled. "*Every* time... there you are. I've come by my own hands more times than I care to keep track of. When I do, I've been thinking of your juicy, perfect mouth...how it would feel to finally kiss it...to sink my cock into it."

I sputtered a little. All his dirty talk was making me gush down below, tying the rest of my insides into a network of tight knots.

"Fletcher." I had a complete thought to add to that, but it slipped away when he nuzzled into my neck and hair, matching the erotic onslaught delivered by his best friend.

Ohhhh...*man*. They were really, *really* good at this. Within seconds, the three of us were tangled in each other's arms and legs. The two of them pressed even closer, surrounding me in their power and heat. It was wonderful. *So* damn wonderful.

"What, baby?" Fletcher's voice, always underlined with a musical quality, was entrancing in its blatant arousal. "Tell me what you want. I'll do whatever you say—except stop. I can't stop now. I've had just a little taste, and now I want more. Your skin, your softness, your smell... They lure me in, Talia. You have me in your spell."

"We shouldn't—"

"We should."

"I'm serious." But even as it spilled out, I tilted my head back, yearning for their seduction to continue. We needed to stop. I had to make them stop. I tried so hard to make them...

Right. And this joint was really a Holiday Inn.

I wasn't trying—at all. It all felt so good...too good. I couldn't convince myself it was wrong, even knowing damn well my family would disown me at once over something like this. If Mama, Papa, and the rest *ever* found out, I'd be a Perizkova outcast the moment the news spread.

But feeling the barely contained passion of these men, one throbbing into me from the front and one seducing me from behind, I could only really process one question.

Now what?

The men moved with sensual, perfect precision, as if reading my thoughts as well as each other's. They functioned almost as one being, shifting and sliding, touching and teasing, growling and encouraging. They were relentless about breaking down my walls, their mighty spirits focused on simply making me feel good.

Fletcher's hands were at the hem of my shirt, toying with my exposed skin and igniting my desire. I willingly raised my arms when he tugged to lift it over my head, leaving me in a yellow and white polka dot bra and my loose jogging pants. His fingers skated up my sides and back down again, exploring the tan flesh.

Drake finally lifted his head from my neck long enough to take in his new view. "Shit. I must've been a very good boy this year. Christmas is here again."

"Hey," Fletch barked. "Sharing is caring, man." He pulled gently on my shoulder. "Tolly, turn on Drake's lap. Face me."

His effortless command had me obeying without question. I swung my legs to the front and then leaned back on Drake's wide chest. The move offered my breasts to Fletcher like a reward.

"Jesus Christ, Newland. You weren't kidding." He raised his hands, cupping me through the fabric of my bra.

It wasn't too late to stop. All I had to do was—

"Oh, my God."

The moan spilled from me almost automatically as Fletcher bent forward and kissed what he could of my breasts, overflowing from the demi cup of my bra. All right, maybe he even encouraged the swell a little, pushing it up with his steady, powerful hand. He licked at my skin, leaving a warm, wet trail across my flesh. I needed more. But just when I moved to grip his head, Drake circled each of my wrists with his fingers and lifted my arms up and back, clasping them behind his head. I was so open and vulnerable now, completely offered up to Fletcher's hungry mouth.

"Fuck, woman." Fletcher's reaction was a chainsaw of

sensuality. "You're going to be my goddamn death. Do you realize what you're doing to me?"

As he reached between his legs, gripping himself through his slacks, my eyes grew wide. Oh, this was...interesting. And so, so hot. I swallowed hard, fixated on the outline of his cock in his hand, straining through the fabric and begging to be set free.

"We—we *really* should stop."

"*No.*" This time they answered in unison. "We shouldn't."

But Fletcher could clearly see the war going on inside my head. There was a mental game of shirts versus skins happening on the playground of my mind, and by the goosebumps breaking out across my flesh, I knew which team I was on. But would winning mean giving in to the ache growing deep in my core or fighting off the pleasure they could give me together?

A sharp pinch to my nipple snapped me from the musing. The pain quickly morphed into pleasure as Drake extended the pressure to my sensitive tip.

"Stay right here with us, baby. No drifting off. No listening to the negative crap you're brewing inside that beautiful little mind."

"I wasn't—" My words were cut off by another pinch, focusing on the other nipple. "Ohhhh, shit. Oh-oh-okay." The last word twined with a groan—as my panties got even wetter.

Fletcher's eyes sparkled with the light of fresh discovery. "Someone likes that more than she can reason through, hmm?"

"No," I protested. "It's just—"

Drake twisted my nipple harder, cutting off thought entirely.

I sighed, breathy and needy. "Okay, ummm...yeah. Th-That feels good."

"Good girl," Fletcher crooned. "Let it go. Just feel us. We will be so good to you."

By now, I was swimming in a lust-filled haze. Instead, I whimpered and sighed, subdued and seduced. I should've still been fighting it. Fighting *them*. It was wrong to feel this good. It had to be.

But this time, my own thoughts were my traitors. While I wrestled through my inner turmoil, Fletcher unhooked my bra and slid the straps down my arms. When they reached my elbows, he stopped. He studied me twice as carefully as before, almost as if daring me to stop him now.

And I couldn't. God, I just couldn't do it. I just...wanted to feel like this forever. Cherished. Desired. The complete focus of two sinfully inviting men. I wanted an eternity of floating in the clouds above my own body. Of feeling every cell as if it had been newly crafted by fate, especially for the purpose of pleasing these men in every way possible.

My bra fell away, and warm hands took its place. My breasts weren't oversized, but they filled Drake's palms with their flesh. He completely appreciated that fact, judging by the leonine growl at my ear and the ridge pushing even harder against my ass. He swiveled his hips under me now, matching the tempo of his hands.

"Fuck me. What a sight." Fletcher moved closer still, plunging in to kiss my jaw and cheeks before finally diving back into my mouth.

I felt like I could get off just from the attention they were both lavishing on me, especially if I angled back a bit. If I ground my clit right on Drake's... *Oh, yeah, just like that.*

A little keening noise came from my throat, making Fletcher pull back from our kiss and smile. "This dry humping you two have going on is making me ridiculously hard. And fucking jealous."

Drake responded with something between a chuckle and a growl. "She feels so damn good, man."

"Asshole," Fletch jibed.

"But we need to take this to the bed. Or the sofa. Fuck, even the floor's a good choice. Talia...baby...I need to see all of you."

Fletcher pulled me forward, off Drake's lap. But when I was up, he kept his arms tight around my waist, balancing me as I stood. Thank God for it. My head buzzed as if I had really turned upside down, and I probably would have stumbled without him. I sagged heavily into his chest, inhaling his distinct, expensive cologne. The man always smelled *so* amazing. Fletcher Ford's scent was all fashion model and high-end department store, the finest fragrance lingering on his skin as if he'd been genetically engineered to wear the stuff. That being said, he was never just a wall of smell when near. He probably used the whole line of products. It was spicy and comforting and so deep in his skin I could burrow my face in his chest all day.

In contrast, Drake was earth and woods, a lot like the cabin Mama and Papa had rented in Big Bear during our winter breaks from school. It wasn't strictly pine, more of a mixture of all the trees and plants that grew up there that we didn't see in San Diego.

I was so lost in my olfactory musings that I jumped when the backs of my knees hit the sofa.

"Easy, baby," Drake soothed. "Just sit down. We want to get more comfortable with you."

Comfortable? They wanted to get comfortable, and all

I could think of was how hot they'd have to make my blood before spontaneous combustion occurred?

On that inspiring thought, I sank to the sofa. They followed, one man on either side—my favorite move of theirs. With a pair of efficient swoops, they yanked free the back cushions and tossed them to the floor behind, growing the "let's get comfortable" depth by two.

"Lie back, sweet girl."

They moved again. Drake scooted to kneel on the floor while Fletcher easily slid behind me. It was a little disconcerting, just how perfectly I fit into the curve of his body when we lay down. Drake reached up, fanning my hair out above us, making me even more comfortable, despite the majestic sight of his power at work. I admired his every move, watching how the muscles worked along the length of his arm. I could only imagine what he looked like underneath his clothes. On the few occasions I'd managed to sneak in a friendly touch, he'd felt like a brick house—the industrial prison cell ones, not the curvy, decorative patio kind. I yearned to learn it all now for myself.

And, apparently, I was transparent about it too.

Drake leaned in, tapping on my temple. "What's going on in there?"

Yikes. Embarrassment—again. I was going to have to get better at hiding my thoughts. Clearly, they ran across my face like a streaker at a football game.

"Nothing." I tried a sweet smile, attempting to distract him.

His forehead furrowed. "You don't have to hide from either of us, Talia. If you haven't figured it out by now, the things we want to do with you are very...specific."

"He means intimate," Fletcher teased. A little. The rest was pure, fluent sexual intent.

"There's no room for hiding or lying when we are all together. You won't get that from us, and we expect none of it in return. So let's try again, hmm?"

Wait. Whaaaa?

No. Uh-uh. I really couldn't do this. If their purpose was to indulge a little fling while we were here in this room, fine. Maybe. I was close to considering it. But after that solemn, stern lecture? *What* was going on? Had they been writing our wedding vows in their spare time? And how ludicrous was *that* to think of, on its own? Wedding vows. As if three people could much less live together in *that* kind of way, let alone put rings on it. As if anyone in the "normal" world would ever be okay with that.

"Seriously, nothing. I was just enjoying all the attention. You two are going to have me so spoiled by the end of this weekend."

Fletcher curled a hand against my face, tugging me around to gaze at him. "You don't know the half of it yet."

His promise was as velvety-smooth as his eyes, drawing me closer until our lips met. He yanked me in closer, consuming my mouth with his own. Okay, so that ceased Drake's cross-examination, but I was now on another hook entirely—and wasn't sure I wanted off. I sank into the kiss, reveling in the feel of Fletch's mouth controlling mine, and tried to let go of all the anxiety.

Well, most.

I really needed to pick one side or the other. Throw myself totally into this sea of lust or run for the safety of the shore, far, far away from these tidal waves disguised as men. I couldn't stay here and even hope to win the battle by talking to them anymore. I was doomed if I stayed, especially with the full talent of Fletcher Ford's mouth now unleashed on me. His lips were so agile and his tongue was so skilled, working its sinful magic all over my cheek, jaw, and neck. I sighed as he pushed up on his elbow in order to loom farther over me, gazing into my face before covering my mouth once more.

My control slipped another notch. I mewled in protest, but it dropped again. Oh, how I wanted to give myself over to him...in every carnal sense of the word. He sucked and nibbled, played and teased. I felt myself drowning deeper...deeper.

Warm kisses covered my belly. So Drake was over his inquisition...and had decided to play with us. Yikes. Was that a good thing or a bad thing? Or did I even need to keep caring? Option two felt more logical by the second while he drew lazy, wanton circles on my flesh...at last ending up along the waistband of my pants.

"God!" I exclaimed.

"Drake will do," he hummed, nuzzling my navel with his nose.

With his teeth, he nibbled my stomach in all the places where I'd normally be ticklish. Nothing about what I felt was remotely funny. I willed him to go lower—silently begged him to continue his path downward. The ache between my legs was palpable, unbearable. I throbbed. I quivered. I lusted.

When he dipped a hand into my pants, I nearly leaped off the sofa. My skin had become so sensitive, all of my blood surging to the surface of my intimate lips as well as the coil of sensitive nerves at their center.

Please don't stop.

The words ran through my head on a continuous loop.

Just don't stop.

He dipped his long fingers beneath the satin of my panties as I pushed my hips up to meet them. "Ohhhhh!"

"That's it, baby. Give it to me. You're so warm in here. So inviting."

I couldn't answer his dirty talk. Not in...specifics. But it didn't really matter. His smile told me as much. It grew, so dazzling and beautiful in his dark face that I pressed my mound into his hand again.

"You're the sexiest thing I've ever touched, Talia. Your body feels so good under my hand. I'm going to make you come this way, with my fingers. Fletcher's going to kiss you and caress you and make you feel good...and I'm going to take care of the rest."

I moaned as he twirled his fingers through my wetness. *Finally.* My clit throbbed in double-time with my pulse, leading the way toward my elusive, perfect explosion. I wanted it so badly now and would resort to any manner of moaning, wheedling, or bargaining for it. I wasn't normally so free with my sexuality, but together, they made me feel safe...so desired.

I reached out to touch one of them. It didn't matter which one. I wanted to feel both of them. Fletcher was first within reach. I moved my hand down his body, learning he'd shifted around enough to let me squeeze his tight ass. He groaned and surged his hips toward me. His shaft was so hard it was almost painful as he ground it against me. I kneaded his backside a little harder, encouraging him to take his pleasure however he could.

"*Fuck*, Tolly." The growl reverberated through both our bodies before he kissed me again, holding none of his desire back.

I understood the intensity of his voice. I'd never been kissed so thoroughly. I didn't want any of it to end...now that I'd resigned myself to really going for it.

Drake kept strumming fingers along my sex. He toyed with my clit in knowing little circles, rubbing slowly, using my own wetness to slick my folds.

With steady boldness, he pushed a finger into me. I couldn't stifle the moan that escaped. It was good. *So* good.

"Drake!"

"I know, baby. It's going to get better. Just relax and let me take you there."

"It feels so... I can't! I-I don't—"

"Ssshhhh. You don't have to do anything. Just enjoy."

I wanted to follow his instructions, but I felt confused when I let myself think too long. What we were doing was wrong, and we still had to get through the launch.

A pinch to the inside of my thigh snapped my attention back up. "Owww! Hey!"

Drake's gaze was now a storm, his face rugged with censure. "Stay out of your own way, Talia."

His voice, clearly meant as a warning, heated my blood in new ways instead. Its dominant resonance vibrated through so many cells of my body, finally settling again...directly under his fingers.

Just great.

Fletcher stayed busy with his end of the arrangement. He sucked his way down my neck, leaving a hot, wet trail in his wake that induced me to even more shivers. As he sank his teeth into my collarbone, I moaned and laced my fingers through his thick, wavy hair. I held on tighter to the glorious strands while pumping my hips in time with Drake's fingers, taking more of what I needed. I promised myself to regroup after the orgasm bowled me down. It was building so quickly, brilliant and bright, and I couldn't have stopped it if I tried.

So close.

So...close...

Fletcher closed his mouth around my erect nipple, and I swore my ecstasy to the heavens. He toyed with the bud so expertly, better than anything I had felt there before. I never knew my breasts could be so sensitive, but I had also never been shown that very pleasurable fact. I gasped and even laughed a little as he twisted his head in, sucking the flesh on the underside. The contact shot sharp waves of pleasure directly to my clit.

Drake emitted a low hum. "She likes that, my brother. She just soaked my hand."

Fletcher didn't answer with words. Instead he kept up that tingling torment, thoroughly exploring the undersides of both my breasts. I moaned before writhing harder on Drake's hand. A fleeting thought broke in, ordering me to be at least a little embarrassed, but it was ripped away as quickly as it'd struck— as Drake plunged a third finger into my dripping entrance.

"God! So good!" It wasn't poetic, but I was over being graceful about this. I would probably have enough time to be ashamed when it was over—why spoil the moment so soon? "Please. *Please*, Drake. Fletcher? Somebody please! I need to—"

"And you shall, beautiful girl." Fletcher stopped long enough to praise me. "Just let it go, baby. Come for us. Let us see you fall apart. We'll be right here to catch you too. Always. Let it take you away."

That was all it took. His beautiful baritone voice. Those

hot words of adoration...and freedom. His sparkling blue eyes, gaining new light while he watched me do exactly as he'd encouraged. The climax hit, intense and unreal. Drake kept pumping his fingers into me with the perfect rhythm, worshiping my clit with his thumb. The pressure coiled so tightly in my belly I shook. Pure arousal sparkled out through my limbs, shimmering brighter than the Strip below us. And it lasted forever. And *ever.* They both kept at me, merciless in their ministrations, until I finally pushed away.

"Please! I can't take any more. You're going to kill me with pleasure. Seriously—whoa."

I had to grab Drake's hand, stopping him so I could catch my breath. He narrowed his eyes, which were dark as the sky outside, to indicate I'd be paying for the move later. So much power bottled in one man... He looked like he could run a marathon, climb a mountain, and still have gusto left over to do whatever he damn well wanted with me. Potent energy poured off him in waves. His chest pumped with each breath, his cock strained at the material of his pants—though I battled to avoid being overly conscious of the latter.

Who the heck was I kidding? I was all too aware of it. And, now, I was supposed to return his favor, right? I was so out of my comfort zone here. I glanced from Drake to Fletcher and then back, desperately searching for what to say. Maybe if I made just a little move, they'd make it easier for me to get through.

"I want to..." I let my gaze drop to Drake's erection. "I should...um..."

Not that it was a horrible chore. God, he was glorious. The bulge pushed at his clothes with visible pulsations, scary and captivating at the same time.

"Ssshhhh. *Talia*. Come here, baby." Fletcher stretched out his arms, beckoning me to burrow against him once more. He was so warm. So hard. So reassuring.

"But...you both just made the world stop turning. You know that, right?"

His chuckle sprang from deep in his chest, reverberating against my ear. "Uh, yeah. We know."

"So...turnabout is fair play, right? I need to—"

My words snagged as I looked out, confronting the fresh intensity in Drake's stare. He eyed Fletch and me like a wolf waiting for dinner. He was so turned on, it appeared painful.

"No," he growled. "You have it all wrong."

I frowned but said nothing. I was further out of my league than I realized.

"This? Tonight? This was all about *you*, Talia. Seeing you come apart because of what we gave you? That was a gift, baby, all on its own. I will replay the sight again and again in my mind, trust me."

I darkened my scowl. "It just seems wrong."

Drake grunted low.

Fletcher wasn't so kind. After a guttural version of some choice profanities, he snarled, "No way. You're *not* going to start with that again already."

"Why?" I tried to lift up, like that got me very far. "It's greedy to just take and not give. I'm not used to it." Understatement didn't even touch that. I wasn't used to *any* of this. Worst of all, what happened to the three of us from here? Our relationship had been irrevocably changed, and things like regret and doubt had already started plaguing my psyche. Could we survive this and make our way back to the easy friendship of before? I'd come to rely on them being a part of my life every day. I *liked* them being there. More than I'd ever even admitted to myself—until now.

"Uh-oh."

I looked up again, jarred from my thoughts by Drake's ominous drawl. "What?"

He reached out, tugging at the ends of my hair. A thick swath had shifted forward to fall over my breast. "Where'd you go, Tolly?"

He used the strands to tickle at my skin, making me uncomfortably aware that I was lying there topless in front of them. I darted a glance around, anxious for something to cover up with, but my shirt was on the floor over by the table, where we'd started this.

"Why do you want to hide yourself from us, love? You are so damn beautiful. I'd be happy if you never put a stitch of clothing on again."

Though Drake asked it, I averted my sight from them both. It was unnerving, how they seemed to know what I was thinking all the time. My feelings of overexposure were suddenly tied to a lot more than my missing shirt.

The dark-eyed bastard growled as if he'd discerned that thought too. "Scoot closer to Fletcher," he ordered while lowering to the sofa and fitting my back against his chest, bringing me nose-to-nose with Fletcher.

Immediately, I felt encased in a muscle-bound convection oven. If such a thing were possible, I vowed to sell it and become a billionaire. Their combined heat was enough to sear my skin—but what a way to go. I went ahead and closed my eyes. If I was going to hell for this, the damage had surely already been done, so why not enjoy being their sandwich filling for a few minutes longer?

As soon as I let out a blissful sigh, Drake hooked his leg over mine, locking me in tighter—and eliciting Fletch's instant snarl. "Get your nasty fucking foot off me."

"It's not nasty. I see my girl every four weeks. Dick."

"Your girl?"

"Yes. My girl. She does my hands too. Best part is the foot massage."

"I don't even know who you are sometimes."

A huge grin spread across my face. Just like that, the old times were back, complete with their strutting alpha bickering and borderline pissing contests. It was so nice to watch them like this, playing with each other like a pair of wild animal cubs, all teeth with very little bite. Maybe my stress about change and damage had all been for nothing...

As soon as my tension waned, so did my energy. Suddenly I was so tired my closed eyelids refused to reopen. I was so comfortable cocooned between them. So warm...

I drifted off to the gentle breathing of the most amazing two men I'd ever encountered. Before falling completely asleep, I wondered what it would be like to recount this evening to Claire and Margaux. On the other hand, I didn't want to be the cause of premature labor for either of them. Maybe it would remain my little secret.

Excellent plan.

Especially as I remembered my real family, beyond the world of Stone Global Corp.

My bliss turned to acid. Weird nightmares filled my unconscious mind. Papa, Mama, and the rest would never understand how kind, loving, and respectful Fletcher and Drake had been to me. My family would never understand that romance didn't always come in the exact same package.

They wouldn't be open to the idea of packages turning up in different shapes, sizes, and decorations. Instead they would be embarrassed and ashamed to learn I had strong feelings for not one but two men—and then they'd cast me out.

Fitful sleep was my immediate punishment. The heavier burden waited for when I woke up.

CHAPTER NINE

I woke up in bed in my own room of the suite, and I was alone. I was still topless, but Fletch and Drake had tucked the covers up around my neck so I was nice and warm. I'd never slept so hard in my life. It was a little unnerving that they'd managed to move me without waking me.

Easy out for the exhaustion—I blamed the monumental orgasm. Just thinking about it again made my skin prickle and break out in goosebumps. Then my memory expanded to include everything that had come before it...very awful pun *not* intended...

Humor wasn't going to relieve me of the stress this time.

What on earth had I been thinking?

Worse, how would I even face the guys—my *bosses*—today? Their mouths had been all over my flesh. Their hands—and fingers—had explored places only lovers should've been. *Real* lovers...which was *not* their new role. I wouldn't fall into that trap. I wouldn't even label this—

This what?

This. That would have to do for now. This—whatever—that was going on between us. There. This. Oddly, it sounded just fine. For now, at least.

I hauled myself into the shower to wash away the incriminating evidence from my entire body. I had two hours before we needed to be in the exhibit hall, and the show started in four. The day would pass quickly while we were busy, but that didn't give me much hope for afterward. I already knew what I would be wearing on the show floor, so getting ready was like being on autopilot—giving my mind lots of chances to wander back to the sofa and what I'd done with Drake and Fletcher there. Over and over *and over.*

I *really* didn't want to go out into the living room. Unfortunately, I couldn't wait any longer. Coffee was no longer an option. It was a necessity.

I opened my door as quietly as possible. If they had stuck with our original plan, one of them would be sleeping on the sofa.

"Good morning, angel."

I nearly stubbed my toe on the corner of the wall. Both men sat at the table, hot coffee steaming from the cups in front of them.

"Sorry. Didn't mean to scare you." Fletcher's smile was sincere. And so flipping sexy.

"C-Coffee?" I managed.

"Over on the counter. I hope it's not too strong. I know you prefer it all pretty."

"Not the first cup of the morning. It will be perfect, I'm sure." I returned his smile, hoping an attempt at normalcy would calm the riot inside.

Fat chance. They both were so irresistible. So sleep-tussled and scruffy-faced. Had I tripped into a television commercial and they were actually models playing their roles of morning hotness to perfection?

"Did you sleep well, Talia?" Drake finally looked up from the *Wall Street Journal* in front of him. His gaze was dancing this morning, a combination of mischief and sex that froze me in place for one perfect second.

"Yes, thank you. I slept like a rock. Must've felt like one to one of you guys too. I'm not sure how I got to my bed without waking up, but...thank you to whoever put me there."

"It was my pleasure." Drake's tone was affectionate but matter-of-fact. "I told you we would do anything to care for you, and I meant it. No way were we about to let you spend the night on the sofa, especially with the big day ahead."

I motioned across the suite with my chin. "But *you* slept there instead." It wasn't a question. The bedding was still piled on the cushions, betraying exactly where he'd spent his night.

"We also discussed that already."

"So we did."

I really didn't have more to add, and the tone of his voice made it clear that it wasn't up for discussion anyway.

"I'm, ummm, just going to finish getting ready. What time are you guys heading down?"

"We'll all go together," Drake stated. "So I think we should be downstairs in an hour. Maybe leave here in fifty minutes, in case the casino is already crowded. It can be a chore getting from one end of this place to the other."

"I'll be ready to go." I raised my mug in a little salute. "Thanks for the coffee."

On the way out, I walked past Fletcher. He reached to grab me, twining a hand around the tie of my robe. Not having much of a choice, I stopped. Glared at him. Well, tried. His slow, naughty grin was a very hard thing to glare at.

"I just can't keep my hands off you, Tolly." His eyes smoldered, matching flames of desire. "I don't think I could for the life of me now."

I unhitched his hand and stepped away. "We need to be professional today."

He let his hand drop the rest of the way. Sadness crept into his eyes, dousing the fires like a summer storm, but he didn't say anything else. I felt those eyes on me, along with the charcoal darkness of Drake's, as I walked to my room, not daring to glance back. They were both still staring as I turned to close the door. I gave them a sad little smile but wasn't sure what I was trying to convey with it.

One step at a time.

It was the only way we'd all get through the day.

And we *needed* to get through this day.

This was our time. Everything we'd worked so hard for...

But even with that thought pounding in my head, I leaned my ear against the door, shamelessly eavesdropping on their conversation.

"Damn it. I had a feeling she would be like this today. All stiff, closed off."

"So what's the plan?"

"Let's get through the launch. It's the whole reason we're here, and if I know our girl, she'll be easier to please later if we do a good job today."

"I hope you're right, my brother. I just have a bad feeling it's not going to be that easy."

Well, I was glad to hear at least one of them was dealing in reality. *Easier to please later? About what?*

That mystery didn't matter. I'd pretty much made my mind up in the shower about those two. Last night had been a once-and-done thing. *Nothing* of the sort would happen again tonight. It was a mistake to have given them the impression we could ever be more than friends and business associates, and now I had to spend the day reestablishing boundaries with them. My gut said I had my work cut out for me. *Determination* could be both of their middle names.

I wore a smart black pinstriped suit with classic black pumps. My Eastern European ancestry paid off in spades, with my naturally tan skin tone complementing almost every color I wore. I'd decided on a plain white blouse to go beneath the jacket, conservatively unbuttoned by only one hole at the neck. I never wore flashy jewelry or makeup, so I was ready in plenty of time, giving me a chance to sit and get in a quick call to Mama. She panicked if I didn't check in every few days, just to make sure things were going well at home.

"Hello?"

"Hi, Mama."

"Natalia!" The natural suspicion in her voice vanished beneath her wave of affection and love. "How nice to hear your voice this morning. How's the trip?"

"It's going fine so far. The show starts in a few hours. Thought I'd check in now because I probably won't have time later."

"Tolly, you just about ready?" Drake's booming voice came from just outside my door.

Mama's gasp filled the line. "Is that a man, Natalia? In your hotel room with you?"

"No! Well, yes. I mean—"

Oh, this isn't going to end well. Not for the girl who was raised in a strict household that was as black and white as they came. For my parents, things were always right or wrong, no in between. They guarded their daughters' virtues like national treasures. We'd all escaped arranged marriages by only one generation. Trying to explain that I was shacked up with two men for the weekend would be completely pointless, even when leaving out last night's intimate details.

"Mr. Ford and Mr. Newland came to my room so we could walk down to the exhibit hall together."

"Hmmm."

At least she didn't launch into a speech about how I needed a good man to take care of me. That a woman should be at home taking care of a family. That had been an all-time favorite while we'd been growing up. I could probably recite the lecture word for word to this day. And while I appreciated that my parents truly wanted the best for me, I needed to live *my* life at some point, to come to my own decisions. That was where the difficult part came in. Life wasn't cut and dried, black or white. It was a crazy, multicolored rainbow with infinite choices. I loved my family dearly but sometimes felt like I was selling myself short by not seeing everything life had to offer.

"Please, Mama. Not now, okay? I need to be on top of my game today, and a butt-chewing isn't going to help."

A huff. Muttered words in Russian. "That mouth of yours. It is from working in a business office, around so many men."

"Mama, I'm going to go. Fletcher and—Mr. Ford and Mr. Newland are waiting for me. I just wanted to let you know everything is fine. I'll be back in San Diego tomorrow night. Okay?"

She gave another long sigh and finally said goodbye. After I hit the red key, I released a heavy breath of my own and rubbed the tension out of my temples. *Dumb move, girl.* How had I thought she'd offer encouragement or bolstering in any way? I'd had this conversation with myself before, and it had ended in the exact same way. I had to make peace with the fact that she'd never understand my career, let alone be supportive of it.

I walked back out into the main room and came to a

screeching halt. The guys were breathtaking in their suits, perfectly styled hair, and freshly shaven faces. Their different masculine scents had me squirming to be beneath them again.

And the most erotic feature of the whole scene? The way they looked at me. Different but equally enticing. Drake's gaze was filled with dark, open lust. I was certain that if we had enough time, we'd be back on a horizontal surface then and there. Fletcher's gaze possessed more appreciation and pride. I instantly knew how honored he'd be to step out by my side today, causing my confidence to soar. The assurance I realized I'd been searching for from Mama? It was right here the whole time.

I closed my eyes for one second and smiled. I needed to remember this moment. Treasure it for the next time I badly needed some lifting up.

Even though you want to return things to the way they were with these two?

Fletcher took the first step forward. His eyes flared and his head dipped, almost like he was approaching the world's most delicious cake and didn't know where to take a bite first. "My God, you are stunning."

Don't melt. Don't swoon. Don't sigh.

Eye roll. Better choice. "Please. It's a business suit."

"But you're the one wearing it. And you are stunning."

"You're too much."

"Take the compliment, Talia. We only speak the truth." Somehow, Drake had moved too. I turned to find him standing within inches of me. The man was surely part ninja.

"Thank you." It came out in an unintentional whisper while I inspected my toes. Their words. Their boldness. Their attention. All so different from what I was used to. And so, so addicting...

Drake unfurled a little growl of approval. "It can use some work, but that was better."

He leaned over to kiss my cheek.

I forced myself to jerk away. "We can't keep doing that. This. You know, what we did last night?"

"I knew we'd circle back to this bullshit." Fletcher's throat vibrated with a rough sound too—permeating the room with annoyance.

I flung a glare at him, refusing to be daunted. "It's true. We all know it," I snapped.

"Do we?"

Nope. Not daunted, no matter how tempted my nerves were to go there. "Well, I do. You two should too. We're here because Mr. Stone trusted us to launch this cosmetics line for his company. We need to stay focused."

"*Mr. Stone* would approve of every single thing that's taken place on this trip so far. That's something you can count on." Drake was completely serious. "And I'm as focused as I've ever been, so don't worry about that."

Though he finished with a flippant half smirk, the rest of his face was still defined by determination. And pure sex. And brutal gorgeousness.

I swayed. Literally. I was conscious of my body drifting in his direction, like he was the magnet and I was the metal, sucked into his field, helpless against his force.

He reached his hand up to gently stroke my cheek. His heat warmed my soul.

"We're going to take this slow, little girl. We won't ever do anything you don't want us to do. Do you believe me?"

I just nodded.

No. Wait. There isn't a this to take slow. No more this, damn it!

Why? Why was I going down this path again? Letting them lead me like two pied pipers to one very stupid rat. There was something dangerous about being physically near them. I lost my focus. Became a mess of hormones and desire and need.

"Talia?" Fletcher walked over to Drake's side, officially blocking my view from anything else but them. "This doesn't have to be a *thing*. Stop overthinking everything."

I huffed. "I'm not—"

"You *are*, baby girl." He pressed a hand to my other cheek. "You have to feel it, Tolly, just like we do. I was there last night, remember? Your body betrays your words. You need to let us help you be comfortable with what we can give you. But you're going to have to give us some hint about the direction you're going when you drift away from us. Let this happen, baby."

I forced a deep breath in before confessing, "I-I don't know what to say right now. I really just want to get through today, then worry about all of this"—I drew a triangle between the three of us with a finger—"after." My face firmed. "Until then, we need to keep it professional. You two have quite the reputations. The thought of being looked at like the dumb girl who fell for your shit makes me sick. I've worked so hard to get to this point. I won't throw it all away over an orgasm—no matter how amazing it was."

Fletcher's smile was so brilliant, it made my chest flip. "Okay. Cool. We can work with all of that."

Drake didn't copy the grin. His brow furrowed and his jaw tensed. "Wait. What reputations?"

I wasn't sure if they really didn't know or if they were just being obtuse.

"Let's get downstairs," Fletch interceded. "The sooner we start on this...obstacle...the sooner we can get to what really matters."

"This launch is what really matters." I whirled on him with a glare, tossing aside the fact that he was technically my boss. If he insisted on thinking with the wrong head right now, then I insisted on bringing him to heel. "If you don't agree, maybe you should stay in the room and rent a few movies."

As I turned and stomped toward the door, Drake groaned from off to my right. It distracted me enough that I didn't see Fletcher advancing from the left, deftly sliding into every speck of my personal space, until we were nose-to-nose. His eyes glittered, leonine and fierce. His chest sawed in and out with every breath.

"You should watch your sexy little mouth. I know you're serious, but you have no idea how fucking hot you are right now. *None* of us will leave this room if you keep it up."

And just like that, I needed to change my panties. Something about the dance of dark and light in his eyes burned me up. For a split second, I considered forgetting the whole product launch and just throwing myself onto his glorious body.

Who are you, and what have you done with Talia?

I swallowed hard and took a step back. Fletcher's nostrils flared wider. I took another step back. Physical distance was my only ally in the room.

"We need to go, or we're going to miss the opening ceremony." I squeaked it out, never taking my eyes from his.

"Dude, bring it down a notch. She wants to do this thing, so let's do it."

Thank God for Drake in that moment.

We grabbed our things and headed down to the casino level. My pulse still pounded so hard in my neck I was certain even bystanders could notice. I followed Drake through the crowd, his wide shoulders easily cutting through the throngs, even at this hour. The Nyte's public areas hopped at every time of day. Fletcher was close behind, taking every opportunity to bump into me, rub up against me, or guide me by the small of my back. To outside eyes, his gestures were innocent, but the heat from his touch flowed straight to my core every time. I was nearly dizzy when we reached the convention center.

"Everything okay, Tolly? You look flushed."

"Yes!" I probably sounded maniacal. "I'm fine."

A glance showed me Fletch's knowing grin. *Bastard.* He knew I wasn't fine at all and fully seized the chance to gloat about it. Drake caught that gist fast enough too, observing his friend's Cheshire Cat smile—and then emulating it. I sorely wanted to smack both of them.

"Everything good?" Drake drawled. "Yes? Then let's go sell some girly shit."

So I did hit him. Not hard but hard enough. "Oh, my God." My fist barely registered against the hard brawn of his shoulder. "You did not just say that, Drake Newland."

The second his name spilled from my lips, a woman's blond head popped up. "Drake Newland?" she echoed. "Oh my lucky stars, it *is* you! I thought I recognized that grin from across the room but just thought my fantasies were working overtime."

I lowered my arm, watching speechlessly as the tall Southern belle plastered her willowy curves all over my hot boyfriend. Instinctively, I dug my fingernails into my thighs, a painful reminder not to say a word.

You have a huge problem, Talia—and it's not that woman.

Oh, God. I'd just called Drake Newland my boyfriend. Silently and privately—thank heavens for *that*—but if I slipped again, I might not be so lucky.

I had to get my shit together. Fifteen minutes ago, I'd demanded that Fletcher and Drake alter their naughty mindsets—but here I was, breaking my own freaking rules in a huge, crazy, do-*not*-go-there way.

Drake didn't help things, instantly melting me with his apologetic glance while disentangling himself from her tentacle arms. "Janelle. Ummm...wow. I didn't expect to see you here. You remember Fletcher? And this is our associate, Talia Perizkova."

Janelle, if that was what we'd call her instead of the fifteen nicknames I'd already picked for her, wrapped herself around Fletcher now. Her ridiculous pout needed its own showroom for spectacle's sake. "Why didn't you two call me when we left Chattanooga?"

"Janelle. This isn't the place for that conversation. We're here on business." Fletcher extracted himself from her clutches too.

The blond woman finally looked over to where I stood. Correction. Practically glared down her surgically perfect nose at me.

"Oh. Right. Business. Well, if you two want to have a little fun when you're done working tonight, I'm in room 1545. Come on up—I'm sure we can pass the time one way or another. You know what they say. All work and no play?"

"Oh, my God." Though I mumbled it under my breath, I had a feeling the guys heard me.

Janelle the Gazelle kept on with her sing-songy oversharing. "Remember what fun we had *last* time? I think we broke every piece of furniture in that room."

"Enough!" Drake barked.

Fletcher calmed him with a hand on his shoulder. "We really need to get set up inside. Janelle...it was, uhhhh, nice to see you again."

"Okay, then! Call me, 'kay?" She walked away, dramatically holding a phone-shaped hand up to her ear, in case they didn't get the message when she repeated herself over and over, disappearing into the crowd.

In her wake, my heart felt weirdly crushed.

The butterflies swirling in my stomach five minutes ago? Now floated down, dead and lifeless, like leaves falling from an autumn tree.

I wanted to throw up. Several times over. I'd been such a damn fool. What on earth had made me think I would ever be anything special to these two men?

These two *players*.

I turned, barged through the conference room doors, and didn't look back. The last thing I wanted to hear were lame explanations about who that woman was to them and all the fun she'd been so eager to relive with them.

The exhibitor check-in desk was well marked. I picked up the welcome kit and then set out for the SGC Cosmetics booth. Nearly every step of the way, Drake and Fletcher were right behind me. Wisely, they kept their man-whore mouths shut.

The overnight team had set everything up the way we'd mapped it out back in San Diego. The booth looked amazing, helping me focus fully on the reason we were here and not their slutty intentions for sideline fun. Getting physical distance from the guys helped a little too.

When they caught up, I was already storing my purse and water bottles under the table.

"Talia." Drake's directive was a quiet growl.

"Just leave it."

"We don't want to just *leave* it."

"We want to explain," Fletcher added.

"This isn't the time or the place." I was all business, and they both seemed annoyed by it. They were waiting, resolution stamped across their gorgeous faces, when I rose again.

Drake was the first to nod and state, "Agreed. But we *will* talk about it later."

"That won't be necessary. You don't owe me anything. Either of you."

Between the check-in desk and the booth, I'd made a decision. I'd leave the show a little earlier than them and catch a cab to the airport. I would purchase my own commercial ticket back to San Diego—it would cost a fortune, but sometimes the cause had to justify the cost—and be in my own bed by midnight. It was a good plan. The only plan. It would also give me the strength to get through the day.

We put our name badges around our necks and braced for the onslaught of buyers, bloggers, and media. By the afternoon, I was actually grateful to Janelle the Gazelle. Her interruption had set me straight. I would knock this ball out of the figurative park and then get the hell out of the stadium. While the crowd was still going wild, I'd disappear into the chaos.

★ ★ ★ ★

"I'm going to get a soda. Be right back to help with cleanup."

I grabbed my purse from under the table and hightailed it out of the convention center. The show had been a major success. We'd given at least five interviews to top magazines, and all of our samples were gone. The brand had been well received, and once people had started buzzing around the booth, the vibe about SGC Cosmetics had been palpable.

Mission accomplished.

Now it was time for me to get out of Dodge.

By the time they figured out what had happened, I'd be airborne.

I was frantically packing my bag in my bedroom when I heard the door to the suite open so hard it slammed against the interior wall.

"Talia!" Drake's voice echoed through the entire suite.

Scary didn't begin to describe it. I think my knees audibly knocked. Holy shit, he was pissed.

"Where the fuck is she?" Fletcher's grumble wasn't any more forgiving.

"Check her room."

Within seconds, Fletcher filled the doorway. I froze, suitcase in my hand, feeling like Sylvester the cat with Tweety's feathers drifting from my mouth. Only, Fletcher Ford was no cute little Granny. He was huge, furious, and thoroughly set on not moving.

"Please," I whispered, though I meant to shout. "Just let me go."

His cobalt glare implied his refusal. "Why?" he bellowed.

"Why are you running from us?"

Drake joined Fletch in the doorway. If the escape path hadn't been blocked before, it sure as hell was now.

"How did you know I left?" And why was that my immediate question?

"You don't drink soda," Drake answered blandly.

I saw the no-nonsense marine side of the man now. "What?"

"You said you were going to get a soda. You never drink soda."

I dropped my luggage. "Well...hell."

"We would've known, no matter what." Fletcher stepped into the room, putting his hand on his hips as he walked. "We know you, Tolly."

"Just as we knew what was going on with you all damn day," Drake added. "We were watching. You don't think we were, but we saw it all. You put on an amazing act like nothing was bothering you, but we knew it was just that. An act." He shifted closer, as well. "Talia...talk to us. Is this because of Janelle? Because she's—"

"I swear, if you say she's nothing, that what you did with her was nothing, I will knee you both in the balls."

Drake's lips twisted. "Baby, please."

"Fuck that! *Baby, please.*" I mocked his tone. "Fuck you both!"

At once I slapped my hand over my mouth. I rarely—make that never—used profanity. Now, I'd yelled it at the top of my lungs. The men's stares grew cautious. They weren't used to hysterical women, I could guarantee that little factoid. No. They were used to soft, compliant, horny women. Right now, I was like a wild escaped bear, and they were the rookie zookeepers tasked with rounding me up. Poor, poor boys. *Not.*

"Okay, you're overreacting." Fletcher squared his shoulders. "Do we have pasts? Yes, we do. Have we slept with other women? Yes, we have. But that isn't news to you, Talia. This morning wasn't the first time you confronted the truth about us being with a woman together. You've known for a long time, and you still agreed to work with us. You still came on this trip with us."

My jaw worked by itself, but no words came out. Yes, shock really could stun a person into silence. I truly couldn't believe my ears. Did they not understand what all that made me look like?

"So...what?" I finally seethed. "You think that because I knew this all along, I was out here just hoping you sex gods would take pity and throw me a bone? Wait. That's *boner*, isn't it?" I volleyed my accusing glower between the two of them. "Is that really how little you think of me?"

I didn't wait for them to answer. It wouldn't make a difference. I was taking accountability, *right* now, for my part in this disaster. Truly, I had no one to blame but myself. Mama's words rang through my mind. I'd let these men disrespect me all this time because I'd been disrespecting myself. I should have pointed in the mirror with my blaming finger, not at them. The disgusting thing was, they were right too. I knew *exactly* what they were when I signed on for this.

"Excuse me, gentlemen. I have a plane to catch."

Fletcher folded his arms. "You aren't leaving."

Drake did the same. "I'll tie you to that bed until you talk this out with us."

"Mmmm." Fletch's eyes gleamed in his otherwise grim face. "There's a vision, all right."

My mouth dropped open again. "The hell you will!"

Drake inched forward. No wonder the marines had loved him. Any insurgent caught beneath that glare probably surrendered without thinking twice. "Try me. Just fucking try me, Tolly."

In a second, I decided against that. Instead, I turned right to Fletcher. "Okay, you're supposed to be the rational one."

Fletcher chuffed. "Says who?"

"Everyone." I shot him a *duh* grimace before plunging on. "So tell me *you* can see my reasoning?" I hoped my subtle flattery would distract him. If I could just slip past the doorway, I had a good chance of outrunning them. Or so I thought.

That was a huge darn *if*—dashed by the man himself as he smirked slowly and shook his head. "Sugar, I'm feeling a lot of things right now—but reasonable is *not* one of them."

I stormed toward the doorway. "Fine. Get out of my way, then."

Strong arms caught my waist while another set of hands scooped up my ankles. I was swept off my feet and utterly helpless within seconds. Ruthlessly, they tossed me onto my perfectly made bed. I bounced once before sitting up—in time to watch them prowling toward me with hunger in their eyes. Ohhh...wow. I couldn't deny how sexy and exciting it was.

And reckless.

And foolish.

And directly against every rationality I'd just preached at myself.

"Stop!" I put my hands out in front of me—like they paid attention. "I mean it! Stay where you are."

"Why?" Fletcher's head cocked to the side.

"You know we'd never hurt you." Drake's tilted to the

other.

"I-I need space! I can't think clearly when you're both near. I get all confused...turned around." I kept babbling because, remarkably, it had stopped their advances. If I kept talking, they would stay put.

So much for that idea. Struggling for more words had cost me a vital second. Both of them made it to the bed and sat on either side. If I wanted to get away now, I'd have to scramble down to the foot. It was pretty much hopeless, considering how quickly they'd managed to put me here.

"All right, angel." Drake twisted around, planting a hand to the mattress close by. "Out with it. Tell us what's going on. The shit with Janelle might have started it, but you sure as hell have run with it. Your pulse is beating a mile a minute. I can see it from here."

While he talked, Fletcher sneaked closer to me. When he was close enough for me to inhale his decadent scent, I pushed away, trying to scoot farther up the mattress—

Only to collide right into Drake's broad, hard chest.

Damn it!

Trapped between the two hottest men who walked the earth. On a huge, pristine bed. For most girls this would be a fantasy come true.

I gave in to a fit of panic.

"It is not!"

That sounded mature.

"He's so right, baby." Fletcher leaned in, pressing his lips against my throat. "It's throbbing. Right here."

I could feel the blood surge into my veins. And wetness surge into my folds. Trouble. I was in *so* much trouble. "Fletcher...please."

He continued to suck on the same spot...stopping just before a permanent mark would remain. "Please what, baby?"

Drake began stroking my thigh, long slow caresses between my knee and hip. I felt his fingers, like individual pokers, through the fabric of my skirt.

"I-I want you to—"

"You don't want us to stop, angel. If you say you do, you're lying."

"I'll bet her pussy's wet." Fletcher eased the words out through a sensual smile. "Probably as wet as it was last night when you had your fingers buried in her."

"You're probably right, brother." Drake used his nails to catch the hem of my skirt and hike it up an inch. Then two.

"This isn't fair." God. My whining voice sounded like a toddler's.

"Fair?" Fletcher frowned, turning even that expression into a vision of riveting gorgeousness. "What's not fair about you feeling good?"

"I can't fight you off when you gang up on me like this." Screw the toddler. Now my voice wasn't just idiotic but illicit, hoarse and needy, caving to the rising arousal in the air. Theirs. Mine. A force nearly impossible to resist...

"We don't want you to fight us off anymore," one whispered in my ear.

"You don't want that either," the other crooned, moving in on the opposite side.

They were hypnotizing me. Bending me to their will. Twisting my resistance into their perfect, eager plaything.

"No," I finally rasped. "I don't."

I gave up. Let pleasure's floodgate swing wide open—and carry me out to sea on its glorious wave.

As soon as I finished the words, Drake sealed his mouth over mine. I met his kiss with equal force, sucking his greedy mouth in with my tongue. He rumbled low in his throat, filling me with the ruthless vibrations and shaking my whole body with the force of his lust.

"You have the sweetest taste," he finally grated. "I could just kiss you for hours."

"Well, I'd have to object," Fletcher teased. "I'm too damn greedy to go hours without tasting her too."

Drake chuckled softly. "Idiot."

Fletcher didn't answer him. Instead, his piercing blue gaze still on me, he murmured, "If your mouth is this sweet, I can only imagine how delicious your pussy is."

I squeaked. Yes, squeaked. What was my alternative, considering how he'd spoken something so forward? Although the images he evoked were nothing short of hot, I was flustered. Screw that. I was embarrassed. I'd never been completely comfortable with a man doing *that*. Luckily, Gavin was so greedy, he'd never bothered with oral sex. But Fletcher was already eyeing the apex of my thighs like a starved man.

Drake's growl conveyed the same deep hunger. "I say we test that theory. What do you think, my brother?"

"I think that's the best fucking idea I've heard this week. This month."

"No." I sat straight up, pushing at Fletch's shoulders with all my might. "You guys, I'm not—I don't want—just no."

Fletcher dragged both my hands beneath his parted, adoring lips. "Ten minutes. Give us ten minutes, sugar...and then if you really want to stop, we absolutely will."

Drake brushed my hair with his lips. "We only want you to feel perfect, Talia. Every beautiful, incredible inch of you."

"Damn straight." Fletcher drew two of my fingers into his mouth. Swirled his tongue around them in sensual worship until he pulled back to gently bite at their sensitive pads. "Every delectable nook, cranny, and curve."

I moaned softly. It was so official. They could talk an Eskimo out of his igloo in the middle of a blizzard. With a reluctant whimper, I sank back down. As I did, Drake slipped free so that I rested against the mound of luxurious pillows. Fletcher followed me back and then instantly covered my mouth with his. His kisses were so different from Drake's, but I was already so used to them both and able to change my own response accordingly. As Fletcher continued to explore my mouth, Drake undid my chaste white blouse, one button at a time. He covered each exposed space with a new, gentle kiss before moving to the next.

When he got to the valley of my cleavage, he nuzzled his nose against my skin. "You smell like heaven. We are two lucky motherfuckers, Fletch."

"Tell me about it." Fletcher lifted his gaze, locking it with mine. "You're a gift to be treasured, Talia. Let us show you the pleasure you deserve.

With that, I surged up to initiate a kiss. They'd gotten me so turned on already. I wanted them to just stop talking and do something...*anything* to make the ache inside me go away.

"Sit up a sec. Let's get some of this stuff out of the way." Drake tugged my blouse from my shoulders.

I sat forward as he asked. Each man pulled a sleeve off my arm, leaving me panting and exposed in my white lace bra.

"So beautiful," Fletcher groaned. "I love the white against your gorgeous dark skin."

"There isn't an inch of you that should be covered right

now."

Drake reached around to my back and expertly popped open my bra. I sank deeper into the pillow cloud, feeling revered as my breasts were bared to both of their openly lusting stares. He slid his hand to my waist, where he unhooked the top of my skirt and then lowered the zipper beneath it. The air filled with the soft clicks of each tooth escaping the captivity of its tab. I hadn't heard many other sounds that were more erotic—as proven by the new pulsation in every tissue between my legs.

Without even thinking, I lifted my rear so Drake could slide the fabric over my hips, exposing the sexy lingerie I wore beneath. I was immediately thankful I'd listened to Margaux's advice about packing a few extra things. The white lace panties matched my bra, something I'd never given an extra thought about until this trip, but I was damn glad I'd made the effort now.

I watched the guys' faces as inch after inch of my skin was bared. A white garter belt and nude stockings accompanied the panties, appearing to be nothing short of the Holy Grail to the men. Each one immediately reached to touch me. Drake rubbed from my ankle to my hip with long, languorous strokes, while Fletcher went right for my breasts. He rubbed my nipples with his thumbs, intensifying the treatment as my tips hardened for him. The sensation was exquisite. His slightly roughened skin abraded my tender buds, adding extra friction. Goosebumps covered my arms and thighs.

"I think these need to stay." Drake glided a finger beneath one of the garters.

"Absolutely agreed," Fletcher said.

"But these..." Drake got up on his knees, yanking on my panties. "These need to go."

If I'd been bashful before, I was beyond nervous now. It had been so long since I'd been bared to a man's eyes like this—Gavin had never bothered to look, let alone appreciate—and now here I was with two and every light on in the room.

"W-Wait. Maybe we can...turn out the lights?"

"No way. We would miss all of the amazing details. I want to see your face when I finally get my tongue inside you."

I searched frantically between them. I wanted it yet didn't at the same time.

Fletcher pinched the underside of my breast, making me yelp and give him a fierce glare.

"Stay right here with us," he admonished. "Out of your head, baby. Understood?"

"Umm...yeah. Oh—ohhhhhh kaaayy." I was unable to hold back my moan any longer.

Drake had started working my panties back and forth over my clit. The friction was breathtaking. Tormenting. Perfect.

"Fine," I finally blurted. "Lights stay on—but you two have to do something for me in return."

I had no freaking idea where the moxie came from. Some bold force possessed me—so the opposite of all my natural instincts right now—but I liked it. I liked it a lot. So I let it take me further, hitching me up on my knees. I turned toward Fletch first, reaching to unbutton his shirt, much the way Drake had mine. I did it slowly, looking into his striking blue eyes the entire time.

"Hmmm." He smiled. "That feels nice."

I smiled back. "Good."

"But how is this doing something for you when you're doing the work?"

I didn't stop, despite my trembling hands. "Because I

want to see you too. And I want to feel you. All of you. Your skin against mine."

I pushed his shirt across his shoulders and then down his arms. His white T-shirt was the only thing that stood between me and my goal...at least up top. I couldn't focus on the rest right now or I'd be a shaking ball of nerves. I tugged the tee out from his waistline and over his head, skimming his muscled torso as I went. I ran my fingers over him again and again, from his belt to his neck, enjoying the satiny soft skin stretched over the ripples of his defined muscles. My mouth watered. I longed to lean forward and bury my nose in the bit of hair on his chest, to drink him in without stopping.

But I wasn't quite that bold yet.

I turned to Drake...but already found him bare-chested.

"Your wish is my command." He grinned, almost apologetically.

I couldn't reprimand him, not while being so stunned and mesmerized by the tattoo wrapping from his shoulder and down his chest before disappearing into his waistband. It was vibrant and beautiful, just like the man who flaunted it.

"This is stunning." I rubbed my fingers over the ink. I'd never caught even a glimpse of this incredible artwork before. It had always been perfectly hidden under his dress shirts. "What is all this?"

"A dedication to my fallen marine brothers. This is the marine logo, and this symbolizes the loss we all faced in the Gulf. I don't know... It just felt right."

He gave a boyish shrug, and if I hadn't been watching him so closely, I would have missed the haunted flash of grief in his dark, expressive eyes.

"It's beautiful, Drake." I grabbed his slightly fidgeting

hands. "Like you."

He leaned closer, bestowing me with an uncharacteristically gentle kiss. After brushing it over my lips, he kissed my nose and forehead before responding.

"Thank you, baby. You can't possibly understand what your words mean to me."

I smiled. My heart swelled at his emotional side, yet another perspective I'd never seen of him. There were so many facets to these men...so many sides that fleshed out the people they were behind their commanding, polished personas. They surprised me at every turn...which made me actually look forward to the turns now.

Ohhh, God.

Was my heart leading me into dangerous territory? I wasn't sure I wanted that answer. I craved them both. Found a hundred new things every hour to adore about them. Oh, I could easily fall for them both.

Perhaps I already had.

Drake's low rumble drew my sights back to his tanned face. "Lie back, Talia," he directed without preamble. "I want to finish what I started."

He threw a pointed look at my panties. I fell back into the pillows again, in time to watch him crawl toward me... preparing to undress me even further. My sex quivered from the new contact of cool air. My stomach flipped in a complete chaos of excitement and apprehension.

"Ssshhh. Nothing you don't want, remember?"

"I-I remember."

"*Angel.* You look like you're headed for the firing squad."

"I'm...just nervous."

Fletcher sidled closer to stroke my hair back from my

forehead. "Why? We want to make you feel better than you ever have. We'll make it amazing, if you let us."

I gave them a shaky little nod. Decided it was best if I studied the ceiling and tried to relax. Sure, and I'd win the damn lottery tomorrow too. Relax and every one of its definitions fled my brain as Drake's heavy hands skimmed masterfully up my thighs and grabbed the small bands that held my panties together over my hips. He tugged slowly.

"Lift your hips, angel. Let me take them all the way off. And breathe, damn it."

I pushed my feet into the mattress and prayed my Jell-O muscles would cooperate with my obedience. They came through, lifting me enough for Drake to strip the garment all the way off.

Fletcher's low snarl broke into the erotic tension. "Fuck. I can smell your arousal, Tolly. It's making my whole mouth water. What?" He shot back a shrug at my horrified glower. "It's true. We've been talking about eating your pussy for so many months, I think I already know what it's going to taste like."

While he distracted me with those filthy, wonderful words, his partner in crime nipped his way down my side and across the slight swell of my belly. He nuzzled into my skin, kissing me over and over.

"This is my favorite part of you so far, angel. I love the soft, womanly curve here...and here...and here. Damn. You're like a treasure just for us to enjoy."

I buried my hand in his thick hair while he continued to lick and tease the skin around my belly button before moving lower...lower...but then turning back. I whined in protest, scratching my nails into his scalp. Drake groaned, clearly enjoying the torment, proving he didn't mind getting back as good as he gave.

And oh, God...how he gave.

I dug my nails in deeper, repeating the move several times as he finally neared the juncture of my thighs. *At last.* My need had built so high I forgot to be embarrassed or nervous about having his mouth on my private parts.

Fletcher busied himself at my breasts, kneading and tugging one side and then the other. Where his hands weren't, his mouth was. His warm, savoring kisses and bites ignited the dizzy feeling in my mind. I was drowning in a sea of pleasure, and the only life ring I was interested in was an orgasm.

"It feels so good," I finally found the strength to gasp.

"What does, baby?" Fletch glanced up from my breast, his eyes like summer, his smile fun of sin. "Tell us. We love hearing it. Tell all those voices in your head to go to hell, and then let Lucifer bring you all the wicked shit we want to hear."

"Everything." It rushed from me on the bridge of a wanton smile. At least it felt wanton. I was breathy and needy...wicked and wild...and I reveled in every second of it. "All of it. More. *More.*"

Drake dipped lower between my legs, bringing his mouth level with my sex. Insecurity nagged despite the illicit words I'd just spilled, but I bit my lip against protesting his presence directly over those sensitive, hot folds. My clit quivered. My intimate entrance convulsed on the air, needing his mouth there...on me. Sucking me. Licking me...

He ran his fingers up my thighs, one hand on each side, joining them just above my neatly trimmed hair. He repeated the motion, each time ending a little lower. Sizzling sensations already shot out from my core, igniting my nervous system with electricity. I couldn't keep still. When I squirmed under his touch, Drake chuckled low.

"Patience, sweet Talia. The build-up is half the fun."

"Says who?" I panted back.

Fletcher joined him in a naughty chuckle. "Is her cunt wet, man?"

"You have no idea, brother." He taunted me more by blowing across my tender flesh...continuing as he exposed the taut bud of my clit.

As I groaned, he laughed again.

"Oh, little girl. Your pussy is so wet, the insides of your thighs are shining. Right here." He swirled his fingers in the moisture on my upper thighs.

I stiffened and blushed. This was so embarrassing. I was... leaking? *Everywhere?*

"Don't be shy. This is a huge turn-on, angel...seeing how aroused you are, knowing we're the ones making you feel this way..."

Even if I'd wanted to retort, I couldn't. All coherent thought exploded from existence as Drake took a lazy swipe with his tongue along the entire length of my cleft, not stopping until he concluded at the top of my mound. He did it with just the right amount of pressure too, eliciting a moan from deep in my throat. I quickly covered my mouth with my hand, aghast that I had sounded so flagrantly in need. Teasing and wicked were one thing; openly sexual was another.

Fletcher yanked at my hand. "Don't hide your passion from us, sugar. When we hear that you like something, then we know to continue doing it. To keep you lost in every kind of pleasure we can bring." He guided my hand above my head, wrapping my fingers around the rail of the headboard. "Hold on here if you need to do something with your hands. But no more hiding."

I nodded, quirking up a smile at him—until Drake took another pass at me with his wicked, talented tongue.

"Ohhh!" I gripped the damn headboard until my circulation was threatened.

Drake growled in approval, swirling around my clit and teasing at its edges with knowing swipes. I closed my eyes and felt every tingle move through my body. He repeated the action until my belly was wound so tightly I wanted to burst.

"Is she as sweet as we thought?" Fletcher watched Drake with hooded eyes.

"Better. You should come try for yourself though. Don't take my word for it."

Fletcher moved down, joining his friend between my legs. The moment was so forbidden, so erotic, I wondered if it was all a dream—until Fletch spread my leg out farther on the sheets. He stared at my splayed body like I was the Madonna. The look in his eyes made my breath seize in my chest. The three of us weren't supposed to be feeling as deeply as we were, but both their gazes reflected exactly what I felt in my heart.

Fletcher finally bent his head—and pressed a kiss right on my illicit entrance. He didn't stop there. I gasped as he sneaked his tongue out, dipping into the opening. My whole body trembled, giving him encouragement to repeat the move. He delved deeper with each wet stab, making my pulse race, my pussy clench, and my body strain.

He groaned in pleasure when I clenched my inner walls on his tongue. "Damn, woman. You're going to make me come in my pants if you keep that up."

Drake emitted a roguish snort, guessing at what I'd done.

"She does have a tight little cunt, doesn't she?"

"I can't wait to feel it wrapped around my cock."

"No shit. Heaven, right?"

"Oh, my God. *Please!*" I wasn't above begging at that point. The more their tongues played around, the more my mind dipped and swerved. I needed to feel them inside me more than I needed my next breath. "Please! Someone—"

"Easy, Tolly." Drake rained a few kisses along my thigh. "All in due time. There's so much more we have to explore. I haven't had my fill of all this sweet honey of yours."

"Please. Just please—before I lose my nerve about all this. I want—I need—please just do it."

Fletcher lifted off for a second. "Don't you love her innocent version of dirty talk?"

Drake growled. "You have no fucking idea."

"Makes me harder...if that's possible."

He finished that by scooting off the bed and reaching for the waist of his slacks.

"Shit," I gasped out. This *was* real. It was truly about to happen.

I couldn't tear my eyes away as he eased the fabric apart, revealing his golden, toned legs encased in sexy black boxer briefs. He slid even those down his hips, pushing them along his legs before stepping from them.

His erection stood proudly from his body, swaying as he crawled back onto the bed. He was much bigger than Gavin— at least from what I could remember, considering I'd rarely seen him in the light. This—him—Fletcher—he was so much better than all those memories. So much more fascinating.

I was especially mesmerized by the shape of his broad, firm head...and reached out to carefully stroke him there.

"That's it, baby," he hissed. "Yessss. Touch me."

His head fell back as I wrapped my fingers around his stiff crown and gently squeezed. His growing arousal gave me courage. I stroked more, running my thumb along the full vein on the underside of his shaft, feeling him jump in my grasp as I did so. I smiled at him shyly—and then tightened my hold.

"I like the way you do that." His voice was deep and husky.

The look in his eyes promised satisfaction. It empowered me to continue with my exploration. I used my other hand to scrape my nails along the inside of his thigh, now knowing how sensitive that area became from when Drake had done it to me.

Drake hustled off the bed to check the nightstand drawer. Apparently he had stashed a few condoms there when we'd arrived. He returned with two little packages in his hand, deftly flipping one Fletcher's way. Fletch snatched it out of the air and instantly ripped it open. I couldn't tear my eyes from him as he stroked himself a few times before rolling the latex over the head and down his shaft.

He gave me his naughtiest grin while positioning himself directly between my thighs. When Drake climbed all the way back onto the bed, he sat near my head and directed, "Let me sit behind you, baby girl."

I was a bit confused but rose up to allow him to scoot behind me. He dragged me between his legs, my back resting on his chest. Though he still wore his slacks, I could feel the definition of his erection pressing into me.

"Am I hurting you?" I looked back over my shoulder.

He smiled in return. "It's a little tight in there right now, but don't worry. I'll get my turn with you soon, beauty. Besides, I'm going to love watching Fletch fuck you."

If that didn't turn the rest of me to mush, little else would.

Gratefully, I sagged against him, welcoming his toying touch on my breasts. His hands were so big and warm, they made me feel tiny and treasured.

"You like what he's doing?" Fletcher's gaze was hooded and hot, his mouth parting as Drake pulled at both my nipples, turning them upward like red jewels of sacrifice.

"Mmmm-hmmm. But I think I'm about to like what you're doing even more."

Fletcher grinned and lined himself up at my entrance. I was scared and excited, not sure which would win the battle.

"Just go slow, okay?"

"Baby, I would never hurt you."

"It's just...been a while. This is a big change."

"I think things are about to change for all of us, love."

He pushed in just a bit, inciting goosebumps across my skin. My nipples were tighter than ever. Drake hissed when grazing across them.

"You are so fucking sexy." He growled it in my ear. "How does Fletcher's cock feel inside you?"

"Good," I rasped. "So good."

Fletcher thrust an inch deeper. My eyes rolled back in my head. I moaned in pleasure, and he moved again, driving farther into my body. He rocked back and slid in again, creating an amazing friction.

"Oh, God, Fletcher."

"Yeah, sugar?"

"It's—ohhh—"

"I know, baby. *I know.*"

"More. Please...more." I ran my hands up his arms, coiling and flexing in order to brace his weight above me. When our eyes met, I lost my breath at the depth of desire I saw shining back at me. Oceans. His eyes were fathomless, sun-drenched oceans.

My begging urged him on. He moved in and out of me in a deliciously slow rhythm. Drake kept kissing my shoulders and neck, whispering the dirtiest of ideas in my ear. I was going to explode from the pleasure they heaped on me in ever-building waves of ecstasy, heat, and seduction. The pressure in my sex rolled and pushed and demanded, spreading and tingling, a flood begging for a shattered dam, though part of me never wanted the exquisite torture to cease.

"Please, Fletcher. I'm so close. Please...ohhh...*stop*."

"Stop? Why would I stop now?" He grinned down at me.

"I-I don't want it to be over yet."

Drake spoke up. "Sweet girl, you think everything ends at orgasm number one?"

"N-Number...*one*?"

"We're not doing our job if you don't hit four, five, or six by the time we're done."

Fletcher joined his laugh to my gasp. "Think of this as your warm-up."

He leaned down, sinking his teeth into my shoulder... sending me over the edge. Every muscle tensed as tidal waves of tingling pleasure surged through, drowning me in liquid bliss that was unlike anything I'd ever experienced.

When I finally opened my eyes again, Fletcher was staring at me with what seemed like awe. "Sweet Tolly," he grated. "That was the most beautiful thing I've ever seen. You, consumed by pleasure. I feel ten feet tall, baby."

"But you didn't—" My protest was cut off by another mouth covering mine.

Drake's taste consumed me. His passionate groan

resounded through my head.

Just as Fletcher's growl warmed the side of my neck. "We're not in a race, sugar. We have all night. It *may* be enough time."

"For...for what?" I managed to get it out past the numbing pulses Drake left behind on my mouth.

"For making sure you remember exactly who's been inside your body—and exactly what we did to it." He demonstrated the point to perfection by stroking fingers along the lips that still welcomed his swollen sex, continuing to move in and out with slow, sensual deliberation.

I shuddered at once. Everything there was so sensitive after my climax. I bucked up into him, thrusting his cock deeper inside me.

"Ooohhhh!"

"Damn. That feels amazing. I'm so deep in you, baby. Do that again. Fuck yourself on me."

I repeated the motion with my hips, driving him deeper, causing me to gasp with each new lunge. He looked very satisfied with himself every time I cried out, perhaps even smug, but I couldn't contain the sound. I'd never been stimulated so deeply.

"Don't hold it back, Tolly. That one little sound... You have no idea what it does to me."

I laughed a bit. "I might have *some* idea."

"Oh yeah? Well, that sound and your tight, sweet pussy are going to make me explode. Would you like that? If I came deep in your wet cunt?"

I could only nod this time. I couldn't bring myself to repeat the words. I couldn't speak the same way they did, though all of it was the most exciting thing to ever happen to my mind and body. They'd taken over it all, and I never wanted it to end.

"So shy. Sweet, sweet Talia." Drake tweaked my nipples again while he nibbled my neck. "Do it, baby. Make Fletch lose his mind."

His words empowered my hips again, rocking up while Fletcher picked up the pace of his plunges. The muscles in his shoulders and neck bunched as he held himself above me. The only place our bodies touched was intensified by its absence everywhere else.

"Baby...I need to come. I'm going to fill you with this load. Take it for me, Talia. Take it all."

"Do it, man."

"God, yes! Please do it!"

He pumped harder and faster, building up to the explosion that was his release. With a terrible, beautiful groan, he set that force free. I wasn't sure I'd seen anything more captivating than his straining body, his passion-drenched face, and his thrown-back head. I tried to memorize every detail of the moment, knowing I'd be coming back to it later.

His dick pulsed against my inner walls as he slowed his pace, letting my body milk every last drop from his. He buried his forehead into my neck. I could feel the sheen of sweat on his skin.

"My God, Fletch. I hope that was as good as it looked."

When he finally replied to Drake, he had a lazy smile on his lips. "Even better." He lifted up to kiss me long and deep, thrusting his tongue in and out of my mouth, reminding me of the motion that had just brought him such pleasure. That kiss was all it took for my core to stir again. I needed to feel this same bond with Drake. It was instinctual.

Fletcher pulled from my body and stood to discard the

filled condom. I rolled to my belly between Drake's legs. His cock made an impressive bulge in the material still covering it. Unable to hold back, I reached up to firmly stroke him through his pants. He didn't argue. Harsh grunts curled from deep within him, and he pushed himself into my hand like a giant, dark beast needing to be caressed.

"Drake?"

"Yes, angel?"

"Please take these off so I can feel you."

"I'd be happy to, love." He quickly pulled his pants and briefs down over his hips and kicked them away from his feet. "There. Now have your wicked way with me."

Panic set in. I never intended to give him a blow job. I'd never done it in my life, and I couldn't imagine where to start, other than the obvious. I had tried a few times with Gavin, only to have him get frustrated and mean and insult me regarding my lack of experience. Ugly memories battled for the stage of my mind until I looked up and saw Drake's beautiful, soulful eyes drinking me in.

"Come here." He held his arms open.

I crawled into them, resting my head on his chest and listening to the strong assurance of his heartbeat.

"It's just about tonight. Just about right here. No one else gets in. No other worries about past experiences, okay?"

I frantically blinked back tears. "I'm so sorry."

"You have nothing to apologize for. But you can be sure if I ever come face-to-face with the asshole who made you doubt yourself like this, an apology will be the first thing out of his mouth. And then blood, because I'm going to beat some sense into him."

"No. No violence. He's not worth it."

"But you are."

The tears were instantly forgotten. I leaned up to kiss his perfectly shaped lips. For a man who often seemed chiseled from a hunk of onyx, his mouth was impossibly soft and inviting. Such a lethal combination, borne out by my wayward thoughts the exact next moment. Once I started thinking of what his lips and tongue had felt like on my pussy, I squirmed against his hard shaft. Drake's responding moan only cranked my tension higher.

"Can you take more, baby?" he whispered. "I don't want to push you, but—"

"But what?" I locked my needy gaze to the mirror of his. Crap. I'd started craving their filthy words like a junkie.

"I'm dying to bury myself in you," he grated. "To stretch your walls like Fletch did. To fuck you as hard and deep and passionately."

I let a slow smile curl my lips. "And I would love nothing more."

He grinned too. "Straddle me."

He pulled me up higher so I could hike my leg across his torso and sit up on him. I felt shy but empowered at the same time. Drake slid his muscular body up so he was resting against the headboard, dragging me along with him. Now we sat with faces inches apart, his erection jutting between my legs, teasing me in just the right spot. I was still wet from my joining with Fletcher, and I used that slickness to glide back and forth on Drake's length.

"Oh, Christ, that feels good," he praised. "Your pussy's so wet and warm."

"Wait until you get inside her." Fletcher was back from the other side of the room.

He stretched out beside us, intently watching what I was doing. Drake halted me long enough to slide on his condom and then grunted deeply as I began the sensual movements once again.

"Enough," he finally growled, hands digging into my waist. "Come here. Lean up a bit, angel."

I complied, letting him position himself at my entrance. I sat back and allowed my flesh to part around his width, groaning when he pushed up into my body. The farther back I sat, the deeper he went. Before I took his entire length, I raised up so he could slide nearly all the way out. At the last second, I lowered down on him. I repeated the same process going slowly, savoring the full feeling inside my tight channel. He kept his grip on my waist, steadying me...controlling me. I might have been the one on top, but Drake Newland was clearly in charge of every move we made, every second of pleasure I experienced.

When I least expected it, he surged forward. Thrown off balance, I toppled to the bed, my head near the footboard. A giggle bubbled up, but I only got out the start of it, overwhelmed once more by his effortless power, his commanding lust. We were separated, but not for long. He barely skipped a beat before plunging his cock back into me. The pleasure from it was enough to make me cry out. I was so sensitive from Fletcher making love to me, but the small amount of pain morphed into more pleasure.

"Ohhhh, Drake. Feels...so...good."

"It does," he answered. "You're so tight...gripping me so good."

"I-I think I need to come."

"That's damn good, angel, because I'm not going to last

long either."

"Told you so," Fletcher drawled, though rough splinters underscored his tone.

I managed a glance his way. He looked like a lazing lion... with a cock already half-erect again.

"I've waited so long for this," Drake declared. "Too fucking long to feel you."

He dipped in, kissing my mouth with such passion I was left breathless. When I opened my eyes again, it was to confront his intense stare, trying to crawl into my head through my eyes.

Maybe even into my heart.

The pressure built in my core as he thrust faster, harder. This was unbelievable. I really did think I was going to climax a second time. I'd never been able to have more than one orgasm a night, but another one built higher and higher, pounding at my clit for freedom. My eyes shot open wider as he hit a very sensitive spot inside, bringing the urge to pee.

"I know, honey, just relax into it. Let it build into the best orgasm of your life."

"No—no, it feels like I have to pee."

He chuckled. "I know, baby. Just trust me. Relax and feel it."

"I'm going to pee on you if you keep doing that."

"No, you're going to shatter into a million pieces if I keep doing that."

Fletcher provided the laugh I couldn't, shifting over to help his friend by brushing my hair back, gently kissing my forehead. "Trust him, Tolly. He knows what he's doing. Let it go, baby."

As Drake kicked up the pace of his cock, Fletcher caressed and pinched my nipples, intensifying the sensations in my clit.

My eyes slid shut.

My body zinged alive.

The sound of flesh slapping flesh filled the room. Every time Drake hit *that* spot, dark spots danced across my vision—and apprehension needled my veins. I tried desperately to do what they said, to relax and let the feelings take me away. Soon, I wasn't conscious of time passing or even my heart beating. My whole world became the feeling of the cock inside me—claiming me, igniting me, branding me. The pressure climbed inside my sex. Higher. *Higher.*

"Come with me, baby. You ready?"

"Y-Yes," I forced out. "God, yes, please!"

I'd surely explode if I didn't get some sort of relief. Drake reached between us and pressed on my clit, so slick and wet now. He rubbed faster, fucked me harder—then, suddenly, something snapped. A terrifying, amazing feeling crawled across my chest, down my torso, and burst from my core in a thousand points of light. I fought just to get air, seized by the most amazing orgasm of my life. Drake roared as he pulsed into me, his own release rocketing through him.

My eyes popped open, wide with astonishment. I gulped down air. Whatever he had just done to me, I wanted to do every night until I died. On the heels of that thought, emotions flooded into my heart. I struggled against revealing them. I wanted to tell him, tell *them*, that I'd fallen in love with them.

Oh, God. Yes. I loved them.

The confession hung on the tip of my tongue, waiting to be called forth—

And ruin the entire evening. *The evening?* No. The whole weekend. Our whole friendship. The basis of our very successful working relationship.

I wrapped my arms as tightly as I could around Drake's neck, pulling him to me. I didn't want him to see into my eyes. He could read me so well. My crazy emotions would betray me.

"Holy fuck," Fletcher muttered.

"Jesus." Drake burst it out between heavy breaths. "That was the best orgasm I've ever had."

Silence. More silence. Here was the part for my obligatory *oh, me too!*

It didn't come. I didn't dare speak a word. Of anything.

"Baby?" Drake struggled to pull up, but I held on. "Talia? You okay?" He reached around to unclasp my hands.

My strength was no match for his. As my arms dropped, I turned my head, not wanting to face Fletcher either. I was in deep water. Sinking. Drowning.

"Hey. Hey, baby. It's okay." Fletcher pulled me in tightly while Drake went to ditch the condom. "Seriously, that was intense, I could see it. It's all right to be emotional right now."

"I'm not being emotional!" My hiccupping crack was less than convincing.

"Then it's okay to *not* be emotional." He chuckled, running fingers through my hair, soothing me while I shuddered.

"That was—it's just that it was so—so much. *So* much."

Drake returned, pulling me back toward the top of the bed. He and Fletcher untucked the comforter and then swept the covers up, blanketing the three of us. Drake urged me into his tight, safe embrace.

"Thank you," he whispered into my hair.

"Why are you thanking me? You did all the hard work." I tried for levity, but tears ran down my cheeks, ratting me out like a grade school tattletale.

"I'm thanking you because you shared yourself with me. With us. And it meant the world to us both. We've wanted you for so long, Talia Perizkova. I can't speak for Fletch, but it was beyond worth the wait for me. I'm already thinking about doing it again."

"Well spoken, brother." Fletcher's words warmed my back and neck as he curled his body against mine. "I couldn't agree with you more. That was the most explosive experience I've ever had. I knew it would be amazing, but nothing could've prepared me for the way it actually felt to be inside you, sweet Tolly."

More tears came uninvited. Why were they being the damn wonder lovers? Sounding so genuine? I didn't need their mind games on top of my heart running rogue.

"Okay, guys. Enough. You don't have to say all of these nice things. I know what this was all about, and I went into it knowing full well where we all stand."

"Where exactly is that?" Drake loosened his hold on me, and I immediately felt the loss.

"I'm not sure I'm going to like this. Something is giving me a bad vibe all of a sudden."

In two sentences, Fletcher summed up exactly why I loved him so much. There was my brutally open man, saying exactly what everyone else was thinking. Judging by the foreboding look that crossed Drake's face when I glanced up, that was definitely the case. I'd struck a nerve.

"Did you hear my question, Talia?" His voice edged on stern. "I said, where do you think we stand?"

There was no getting out of this. And maybe it was just as well that I laid it on the table for them. They could stop faking feelings they weren't feeling, and hopefully we could all walk away from this with our dignities intact.

Not to mention our hearts.

"All right, fine." I huffed. "I know all about your lifestyle, gentlemen, if we can call it that without getting crass."

Fletcher grunted. "You mean our sex lives? Just say it, sugar. *Sex*. It's not a bad word. Actually, I think we all just proved it's an amazing word."

"All right, fine. I know all about your sexual preferences. And everyone knows people can't be in a relationship if there are three people in the bed all the time. This is what people do to scratch an itch—let loose a little bit, cross something off their bucket list."

"Bucket list?" Drake tacked his stare over me to Fletch. "Did she really just say that?"

"I think she did." He snapped it while standing up and pulling on his trousers. Only then did he bolt his stare back down at me. "You did all this just to mark something off your bucket list?"

Without waiting for a reply, he glanced back at Drake. They exchanged a look I couldn't quite distinguish, but if I had to label it, *furious* jumped to mind.

And men claimed *women* were confusing?

"Why are you so upset? I thought this was the way you guys worked."

"The way we worked?" Drake also shot from the bed, grabbing for his clothes.

I sat up in the middle of the rumpled sheets, hugging the top one to my chest. "What am I missing here? You can't seriously tell me you came into this weekend wanting anything more than a roll in the hay."

Drake whirled back around, eyes dark and stormy, his

desire of minutes ago now eclipsed by anger. "Why? Because that's all we're capable of? Hell, we couldn't possibly have *feelings* for you, right? After all, you have this totally figured out. I'm impressed, Talia. Really fucking impressed."

Fletcher rounded the foot of the bed. "Dude, stop. If you say something you can't take back—"

"Fuck that. I'm pissed. And for the first time in my life, I feel used. I really did go into this weekend wanting more than a fling. I have actual real-life feelings for you, Miss Perizkova— but I see now that I was mistaken when I thought you felt them too." He buttoned up his shirt with scary speed and precision. Raked a tense hand back through his thick hair. "I'm going downstairs to the bar."

"Wait up, bro. I'll come with you. Suddenly, I could use some air too."

"Wait. *Wait.* What the heck is happening here?" My whole body shook. Panic stabbed, merciless and cold. Clearly I had misunderstood their intentions. Misunderstood? How about completely misjudged? But now they were both so angry, I was too nervous to even try to talk it through.

"You can have exactly what you wanted. I hope it was good for you, Talia." Drake grabbed his wallet off the dresser and walked out of the door.

Fletcher followed but not without looking back at me, sadness turning his eyes the color of a robin's egg. It made my chest physically ache.

What have I done?

The door onto the outside hall slammed. The ensuing silence pricked instant tears to my eyes. But I sucked in a fast breath, combating the loss. I refused to sit in our little love nest and feel sorry for myself.

I stomped into my bathroom and ran the water in the tub. A few minutes later, sinking up to my neck in the lavender bubbles, I tried to analyze the night.

Drake Newland. Fletcher Ford. They were amazing lovers, the best I'd probably ever have. They were both filled with such passion and tenderness. The thought of losing them felt like an elephant sitting on my chest. I rubbed the spot over my heart, striving to massage the pain away, but nothing worked. I closed my eyes and breathed deeply, but the pain persisted. I'd screwed up, and it would haunt me for the rest of my life. I'd been given not one but two men who cared for me like nobody else ever had, and I'd blown it. Sent them running for the hills before we even stood a chance.

Mama's face came unbidden to my mind. Her nagging voice lectured into my miserable haze, chastising me about allowing this situation to happen in the first place. It served me right to be hurting. I'd brought it on myself. If I'd been acting respectably, I would have been respected.

But they *were* respectful. Beyond that. They'd caressed away my stress. Knew how I liked my steak. Even on the exhibit hall floor, they'd treated me as an equal voice, a valuable business partner. And in their lovemaking, they'd redefined kind and loving and generous.

What the hell have I done?

I needed to apologize. As soon as they came back to the room—to see if there was any hope of salvaging all the feelings we'd unleashed not two hours ago. If it had all been real, it couldn't just be turned on and turned off so easily, right?

I hauled myself from the bath, feeling like I'd forged a plan. I'd do it. Would grovel and plead if I needed to. If nothing else, I still wanted Drake and Fletcher to be my friends. I enjoyed being with them so much. What would my life be like without them at all? I wasn't ready to let go and desperately hoped they felt the same way. Maybe we could recapture what I'd just ruined. I wouldn't know unless I tried.

I fell asleep on the end of my bed, door wide open, waiting for them to come back. My body was sore and tender in the most delicious ways, and I took comfort in those memories until I could fix everything else.

They had to understand that I was just confused.

They just had to.

CHAPTER TEN

Sunlight warmed my face, waking me gently from a restless night of sleep. I still lay across the foot of my bed, but someone had covered me with a blanket. My door was open, and the windows in the living room glowed with the morning desert sun stretching across the suite, shining into my room. I listened for voices or movement, but the place was still and quiet. It was well past midnight the last time I remembered checking the clock. I wasn't sure the guys had come in at all.

I wrapped the plush robe around myself and sneaked out into the kitchenette to make some coffee. Drake was softly snoring on the sofa, so I tried to be extra quiet. When the coffee's aroma filled the room, his eyes popped open.

I smiled shyly, trying to gauge if he was still angry. "Want some?"

"That would be great," he mumbled, rubbing his eyes and stretching. I couldn't tear my eyes off his fit body as he worked out the kinks from sleeping on the sofa. Guilt coursed through my heart. I should've insisted on sleeping there at least one of the nights—though last night I was in no position to be insisting on anything.

After working with the man for months, I knew Drake drank his coffee black, so I walked over to the sofa with a cup in each hand. As I stretched to hand off his mug, steaming coffee splashed over the rim and onto my wrist.

"Oh shit!"

He took his mug while I blew on the redness.

Quicker than I could track, Drake set his cup down, grabbed my unburned wrist, and towed me to the sink. He ran the cool water, feeling it several times with the back of his hand before thrusting my wrist under the stream.

"You should be more careful." He seemed annoyed.

"I'm sorry. It just happened."

"It was an accident, Talia. You don't have to apologize for things you weren't in control of."

I turned off the water and blotted my skin with a towel.

"Maybe not, but I do need to apologize for things I brought on myself. Drake, can we sit down and talk? I really want to set things straight."

"It's okay."

"No, it's not."

"You don't have to."

"No, but I want to. I *need* to."

"Need to what?" A shirtless Fletcher walked out from his room, just as ripped and golden and gorgeous as I remembered from last night. "Is that coffee I smell?"

"Yes, I made a pot. Sit down, and I'll get you a cup. I really need to talk to the two of you."

"You sit down, and I'll get his coffee. You already have one burn."

"You burned yourself? Where? When? Are you okay?" Fletcher's expression suddenly tightened upon his recognition of how he instinctively cared about me.

"She's fine. It's minor. Just a little red now."

"He's right. I'm fine. But will you two just let me say a few things? After that, you can decide what you want to do. If you want me to fly home commercially, I'll understand."

We all sat around the low table and nursed our coffee. Finally, I gathered the courage to say something.

"First of all, I owe you both an apology. I was being ridiculous last night, and I hope you can forgive me. When we were in bed together after—well, you know, just after—I was so flooded with emotions, I got scared. That's hard for me to admit, but that's basically what happened. So instead of risking my heart getting hurt, I trivialized what we had just done, and that was wrong. It was so wrong."

"Why are you saying all of this now?" Drake was skeptical, and I couldn't blame him.

"Because when you guys left and I had the entire night to figure out what was going on in my head...and my heart...I realized how foolish I had been. Now, all I can do is apologize and hope you can forgive me. I didn't mean to hurt either of you. Ever. I think I'm just in way over my head."

"Last night went from so good to so bad, and so quickly. I didn't understand what was going on. It was a merry-go-round of extreme emotions." Fletcher leaned forward, elbows propped on his knees and listened, waiting for my response.

I forced down a deep breath. "I know, and I'm so sorry. I was overwhelmed. I didn't expect to...*feel* as much as I did. I don't think I wanted to."

Drake asked another very good question. "What does that mean? You didn't want to?"

"It means I'm feeling things for the two of you that I'm afraid of. My last relationship wasn't very—oh, what would be a good way of putting it?"

"Were you abused?" Fletcher growled it, always the protector.

"Not physically." I winced. "Well, I guess that's not exactly true either. But mostly emotionally. And mentally. Gavin did a number on my self-esteem and confidence, especially in the bedroom...and with my ability to understand my own feelings. The ones he let me have, at least." I nervously fingered the handle of my mug. "It took me a while to believe in myself again, to be able to trust my own heart."

"We need to kill the bastard."

"My thoughts exactly." They fist-bumped over the preliminary plan.

I shook my head. "He isn't worth either of you getting into trouble or risking getting hurt."

"*Pfffttt.*" Drake scoffed. "Marine? Remember?" He thumped the center of his chest with his thick thumb.

"How could I forget?" I giggled and winked at him, unable to help myself. He was adorable when he was chivalrous. "So, in all seriousness, I want to ask for your forgiveness, for my words and my behavior."

Drake leaned over and tucked a wayward strand of hair behind my ear before letting out a weighted sigh. "I really appreciate your sincerity. I do. Last night was amazing. We'd both fantasized about being with you for so long. When it finally happened, it was better than either of us dreamed. If we're coming on too strong, too fast, can you just promise to let us know? But, baby—we don't want this to be the end of the line. We want to see you and be a part of your life when we get back to San Diego. You know that Fletch and I have always dated women together. It's because we want to be with a woman together for the rest of our lives. This isn't just a game to us. This is what we want. And you're *who* we want."

I stared at him, his words cocooning me in warmth but also overwhelming me a bit. They were willing to forgive me! I wanted to hug them both, but I could sense they needed to be heard as well.

Fletcher stood, walked over, and sat beside me. He took my hands in his and looked into my eyes. "We don't need to hear the words I love you right now, but we do need to hear you say that you will give this a try. Give *us* a try. We want to be with you, Talia. Just you."

"I don't know what to say other than I want to see you too. I've gotten very used to having the two of you in my life. I'm not ready to give that up yet."

"I think we can work with that. D?"

"I think that's a great place to start too."

We all stood, and they wrapped their arms around me, making a tangle of bodies and arms. I felt like I was the luckiest girl on the planet.

"Can we please go home now?" The last thing I wanted to do was get on a plane, but at least my heart felt much lighter. The sooner we got back to San Diego, the sooner we could get on with our lives.

"Let's pack up, and I'll call down to the desk for bell service. I'll have Wesley handle the spa appointments too."

About an hour later, we were heading toward the front of the hotel to meet the driver who would take us to the airport. The guys called the pilot and told him we were leaving a bit ahead of schedule, but the man assured us it was no problem. We moved through the casino, hand in hand in hand, until getting caught behind a human traffic jam in front of a giant, lighted wheel, spinning around and around while people stood cheering for the number they'd bet on.

"What is this game?" I asked Fletcher curiously.

"Simple game of chance," he shrugged. "You put money

down on a number, and the dealer spins the wheel. If your number comes up, you win." A grin spread across his sexy mouth. "What's your lucky number, sugar? Let's try your luck really quick."

I scrunched my face and pulled away. "Oh, I don't have a lucky number."

A mischievous gleam sparkled in his eyes. "Oh yes, you do, Tolly. It's three. You just haven't fully accepted it yet."

Drake smirked. "I like that strategy, brother."

Fletcher flipped out a twenty-dollar bill and placed it on the number three. The dealer let the wheel fly. We watched it go round and round, slowing down incrementally until it finally came to rest...

On the number three.

Fletcher leaned down and kissed me soundly on the lips. "No lucky number, huh?"

Drake wrapped his arm around my waist on one side, Fletcher on the other, and we headed home...together.

Continue Secrets of Stone with Book Six

No Simple Sacrifice

Available Now
Keep reading for an excerpt!

EXCERPT FROM
NO SIMPLE SACRIFICE

BOOK SIX IN THE
SECRETS OF STONE SERIES

CHAPTER ONE

FLETCHER

Should auld acquaintance be forgot...

My ass.

I repeated the sentiment beneath my breath while turning in my chair to stare over the San Diego skyline. The sun glinted brightly on the city's more modern buildings, darkening along the terra-cotta curves of the older structures, crafted in the style of the classic California missions. Farther in the distance, the light sparkled across the gentle waves on Mission Bay.

Shiny, shiny, shiny. Everything and everybody was so happy. They all kept saying it, too. *Happy New Year. Happy New Year.* It was almost February first, and still everyone was going on and on about the happy new year.

"My ass."

Saying it out loud didn't help a damn thing—nor soften the memories taunting me again. It *had* been a happy new year—at first. I'd welcomed it in the best of ways—with my best friend, Drake Newland, and the woman of our dreams, wrapped in our arms at an intimate party for three. A night to remember. A woman to *never* forget. Talia Perizkova—with her huge brown eyes, her dark waterfall of hair, and her perfect temptress's body—had completely captivated Drake and me during one unforgettable night in Vegas...but since then, neither of us could nail her down for an encore. She'd escaped us like a frantic kitten, stopping only long enough to gather traction and run even further. Every time either of us had reached out, she'd had an excuse at the ready. A late-night project at work. A pre-planned event that simply *had* to be attended. Hell, even that she had to wash her damn hair. Fuck. Was that one still around?

Events and projects and dirty hair. All handled—*without us*.

That bullshit ended now.

I wheeled back around to the desk, picked up my phone, and texted Talia with a simple request. We weren't taking no for an answer, and with Drake's buy-in, I was running point on her track-down.

> *Where are you, and when
> can we see you?*

Straight to the point. That was my style. The woman should know that by now—as well as my expectation of an immediate answer. After a minute, I raised an impatient eyebrow at the screen, willing her to reply. When the phone went completely dark, I mentally composed a follow-up—not so nice this time.

The device vibrated in my hand. *Thank fuck.*

Pretty Princess Party Perfection

"What the hell?"

Care to elaborate?

LOL. My niece's birthday party.

*Okay, that makes more sense. When
will you be done? We're coming over.*

*These things can take a
while. Becoming a princess
is time-consuming work.*

*Text us when you get home.
No more excuses, Tolly.*

*Excuses? I would never joke about
dress-up and hairdos.*

I jerked up my other brow. There were two things I'd
learned about Miss Talia Perizkova in the past month. One—
she was a master at hiding her true feelings. Two—she had the
sweetest pussy I'd ever put my mouth on. "Damn," I growled,

fighting thoughts of those tender pink folds beneath my tongue. Complete waste of time. I was a goner, subconsciously rubbing my semi through my slacks as I stood and crossed the room.

I exited into the condo's sprawling living room. Technically, the place belonged to our buddy, Killian Stone, but we were both sitting board members at Stone Global Corporation and had been heavily involved in launching a number of their subdivisions lately. Though we always stayed at one of SGC's rental properties while we were in San Diego, this place was beginning to feel more like home than Chicago—especially since the Talia effect had taken hold. And that was completely fine by me.

Though at the moment, nothing was fine about that girl's diversionary tactics.

Drake was definitely going to agree.

I went looking for my roommate, starting with his favorite room in the condo, the gym. *Condo*. Still felt ridiculous, calling this place that, as it was four-and-a-half thousand square feet of modern, top-of-the-line luxury. Killian's decorating preferences were all over the place, a bit shocking since he usually let *Mrs.* Stone—a.k.a. the amazing Claire—handle the pretties in his world. Still, as Claire's pregnancy gained momentum, Kil was treating her more and more like a china doll instead of a capable, healthy woman. On more than one occasion at the office, we'd all borne witness to the daggers she shot him from her frustrated glares—looks that would've castrated a weaker man. But Kil had left us all slack-jawed by simply managing his trademark grin and then popping a tender kiss to her forehead, making the woman melt into his side. The pair had what most people dreamed of in a relationship, and the envy in the room was usually palpable.

Which—surprise, surprise—circled my mind right back to Talia. Seemed like most things did these days. Again, not a news flash. This was getting...disconcerting. And unnerving and amazing. And thrilling...

And terrifying.

I couldn't remember having been so consumed by a woman before. I was pretty damn sure Drake echoed the feeling.

"Did you track her down?" The man's question shook me out of my mental shadows.

"Uh...yeah."

Drake cocked his head while reseating the dumbbells in the rack. "Are we playing 'I've got a secret,' or are you going to tell me where she is?"

Patience was not Drake Newland's best virtue.

"She's at her niece's birthday party. She doesn't know how long it will go, so I told her to text us when she's home."

"Did she say she would?"

I grimaced. "No. She did her usual bit. Some cutesy quip and then radio silence."

Drake wiped a towel down his sweaty face. "Fuck. This."

"Eloquently put."

He hurled the towel into the hamper. "Well, did she say where the party was?"

"Uh..."

"Yes or no, man?"

"Yes. She *did* say where it was. But—"

"Great." Drake started toward the door of the gym. "Let's just go there. Surprise her." He pulled up short when I didn't budge. Took in my pristine white shirt and dress slacks before offering, "After I shower and change. Happy?"

I shook my head. "We...uh...may want to sit this one out, bro."

"*No.*" He blocked the doorway to the hall. "I'm not waiting anymore. And why are you being so cagey? She needs to realize she can't keep yanking us around like this." He spun and marched down the hallway. "I'll be showered and ready to leave in twenty minutes."

"Ohhhh kaaaay." I wanted to protest again, but his retreating back left no option, so I just grinned at my reflection in the long, mirrored wall. If this went down the way I predicted, Mr. Marine was about to spend the afternoon getting the finest princess makeover a guy could ask for, complete with sparkly nail polish and a fairy-dusted hairdo. This would definitely be my next Snapchat story.

By the time we headed out in the piece-of-shit rental we were driving around and pulled into the strip mall down the street, my phone was out and set to camera. I waited, poised with the thing, ready to capture his face when the realization fell into place.

Didn't take long.

"Fletch, what the fuck is this?"

I shrugged. "Told you we may want to sit this one out."

He grunted. "You must have given me the wrong address. Look it up again."

"No, man, this is it. Pretty Princess Party Perfection."

"Seriously?"

"Seriously." The smirk came out. I just couldn't help it anymore. "Let's go get our girl."

"Ahhhh...maybe you were right. Maybe we should wait." Oh, the gears were clicking fast in his mind now. Girls. Not the fun grown-up kind. The soda-and-cake-filled, hyper-on-life kind. Lots of them. Screaming, giggling, twirling. and reveling in their miniature diva status for the afternoon—primed and ready for a new victim.

He restarted the car.

I reached over and turned it off. "No tucking tail now, man."

"Fuck you."

I hopped out of the car. "Tsk tsk, Prince Drake. Such language." I patted the top of the car before slamming the door and calling over my shoulder, "Suit yourself. I'll be happy to have some time alone with her."

"Fuck that!" The driver's-side door opened and then slammed. Shitkickers pounded the blacktop behind me. Though Drake was a fashion plate at the office, always in head-to-toe custom-fitted suits and dress shirts, he fell back into his comfort zone at home. His penchant for fatigues was legendary. Any camouflage print would do, despite how I cringed every time he put a pair on. Today, thank God, he'd had the sense to go with a regular pair of jeans.

I pulled the door open to Party Perfection which was painted to look like an old wooden door of a castle.

Well. It was a party, all right.

I wasn't sure I'd ever forget the sound. Translation—the decibel-record-setting noise, trounced only by the bright pink-and-purple décor.

And the girls.

Everywhere.

In all sizes, from baby ones to teenaged ones. Some preened in pink salon chairs, getting their hair curled and twisted and sprayed. Some sat on large, ornate thrones with small tubs attached to the front, soaking their feet for their upcoming pedicures. Others riffled through racks of clothing, searching for the perfect princess attire. The ones who were ready for their fashion show were vamping it up on a mini runway lined in twinkle lights and twirling in a sea of disco ball sparkles.

My head was already spinning worse than that damn ball. I wondered if Drake's was just going to explode right off his shoulders. What the hell had I gotten us into? And would we ever find out before the estrogen overload killed us?

"Good morrow, gentlemen!" An overly made-up girl at the reception desk sounded just as sugar-pumped as her clientele. "Are you lost? The tackle shop is three doors down on the—"

"No." I leaned against the counter and poured on the charm. "We're looking for the Perizkova party. We're friends of one of the guests." In went a smooth smile. Couldn't hurt. The last thing we needed was to be tossed out.

"Interesting." Blink. Blink. Then she just stared.

Drake's patience was even thinner than normal. The man looked as though he would rather wrestle a pit of cobras than hang out in here another minute. It certainly wasn't the time to bring it up, but it was one of the funniest things I'd ever seen. Where I was semi-used to this sort of event, because of my extended family, his sister and brother were both still single.

"If you could just point us in the right direction?"

He might as well have left off the question mark—though three-inch-thick-makeup girl seemed to enjoy his demanding tone. She eyed him up and down before grinning. "Sure thing, milord. Follow me. They're in the back, at the makeup stations."

We wove in and out of little princesses as we followed her to the back of the store. Six tall purple director's chairs stood in a row, facing brightly lit mirrors. Each one had a young girl anxiously perched in it, with another woman working diligently on her makeup. There were giggles and whispers as we came to a halt near the first seat.

"Is your friend here?" The receptionist tried to crank down her skepticism while keeping her roving eyes all over Drake.

"Oh. My. God."

Huzzah. We'd been spotted by our very own princess.

"*What* are you two doing here?" Talia bit out.

For a second, I didn't say anything. Couldn't. *Fuck.* The woman was even more breathtaking with bright purple eyeshadow, glitter butterflies in her hair, and a lopsided crown atop her head.

Drake, thank God, hadn't let his head explode yet. "We came to see you." He stamped out each word, openly daring her to challenge them. "You keep blowing us off, love." He shrugged matter-of-factly. "So, *we* came to *you.*"

Talia's eyes grew wide. "I haven't been blowing you off!" She walked over to where we stood—creating a wall of man so she couldn't escape. "And *stop* calling me that!"

I slanted my head toward her. "Are we there again? I thought we handled that in Veg—"

"Ssshhh!" Her eyes weren't just wide anymore. They looked terrified. "Can we...*not* mention Vegas right now?"

Drake turned a little, getting her back against the wall. A flock of sparkly butterflies appeared to be flying out of her head. "Why shouldn't we mention Vegas?"

She popped up on her toes, darting anxious glances around the room. "This isn't the time or the place. My entire family is here, okay? Well...the females, at least."

Drake emitted a low rumble. "So we've noticed."

Talia took that in—and then suddenly burst into laughter. Just as instantly, my dick twitched. She really sounded as magical as a fairy princess.

"All right. I'll bite," I murmured. "What's so funny, Tolly?"

"The two of you. Standing here. In the middle of all... this." She waved her hand through the air to encompass this. I grinned, unable to help myself—deciding that was my favorite habit of hers. The way she waved her hands in the air when she was excited about something... It encompassed so many wonderful things about her personality. Her passion, her life...

But shit. Also her anger. Yeah, she definitely did the hand-waving thing when she was pissed too—especially after the weekend we'd spent together in Las Vegas. Damn, that weekend. The two nights and three days that had changed absolutely everything about the three of us.

I didn't want to see her pissed again for a long time.

Thankfully, now wasn't going to be that time either. Mischief actually began to twinkle in her eyes, forming adorable gold flecks against the sable hues. "Well, gentlemen. You're here. Perhaps you'd like to join us?"

Drake took a turn at the flustered thing. "Uhhh...wh-what do you...?"

"Hey, I can't leave until the party is over, and that's not for another"—she swept her phone screen, checking the time—"two and a half hours."

That was when I saw her game. Little sneak. She was actually banking on us leaving. I stepped up with a smooth-as-Astaire sweep, beating Drake to the answer. "We'd absolutely love to stay, baby. If you're sure the birthday girl won't mind?"

Cue the birthday girl.

"Auntie Talia?" A little girl walked up and studied us with

eyes that were stunningly like Tolly's. The little princess's hair was pulled up into a bunch of elaborate curls, from which turquoise and purple extensions dangled. "Are these your boyfriends?"

"Yes."

"No."

We all answered in unison. The little girl inspected Drake and me as we stared at Talia—daring her to change her response.

"Anya, these are the men I work with. They're friends of mine." Her eyes never left ours, especially as she stomped on the word *friends*. Little minx—always pushing.

Though apparently, in her own way, Anya was on *our* side. "Well, they should be your boyfriends. They're cute and"—she dramatically whispered the last part—"I think they like you."

Drake and I traded smirks. Anya was a smart little thing for...what? Seven? Eight at the most?

"I like this kid," Drake mumbled.

"Agreed," I said.

"Shut. Up," Talia gritted.

I squatted down to be on the birthday girl's level. "So, it's your birthday today?"

"Well, yes. Kind of. This is my party, but my real birthday was on Wednesday, but Mama said we couldn't do the party on a school day, so we had to do it on this day."

I lightly grabbed her white-gloved hand and bowed my head over it. "Your mama sounds like a very smart lady."

Anya giggled. "You can stay if you want! Please say you will." She turned a look up at Talia. "Auntie, don't be rude! Tell them they can stay. They can play with me and my friends!"

"You and your—" Drake choked off the rest of it. As Talia

and I swallowed back chuckles, he spluttered on, "Uhhhhhh... hey...we don't mean to intrude, little one."

"Princess Anya," the girl pointedly reminded him.

"Right. Okay. Well, we just wanted to talk to your aunt for a minute or two."

Talia clenched her jaw. "Two," she ordered, flashing more of those gold knives in her eyes at us both. "*Maximum.*"

"Nonsense." The source of the interjection walked over on graceful steps. An elderly lady, so strikingly similar to Talia that her identity wasn't in doubt, pushed closer to sweep glitter off Talia's nose. "Natalia! Let your friends stay a while. You have better manners than that."

There'd been nothing wrong with the woman's tone— except a full-blown case of maternal chastisement. Instantly, Talia's shoulders sagged. Her gaze swung to the floor. Drake and I exchanged a tight look, filled with the same conclusion. This was something we'd never seen from our forthright, confident Tolly before. Only years' worth of proper training could've done it. As in, a whole life's worth.

"Mama, these are my colleagues, Mr. Drake Newland and Mr. Fletcher Ford." She waved her hand toward each of us during the formality, seeming to appease her mother while making *herself* five times more uncomfortable. As she spoke, several more women converged on the spot where we stood, curiosity painted across their faces.

Talia rolled her eyes and continued with the introductions. Sisters, sisters-in-law, a few aunts, even her grandmother. By the time she was through, I was hoping we wouldn't be tested on any name recalls—especially because so many of them sounded the same. Silver lining? Talia's accent, so fucking sexy as she pronounced each one, made my slacks tight again. I'd have to keep that new discovery in mind for when Drake and I next got her alone.

"So, these are the men from your work? And from the hotel room in Las Vegas?"

I was tempted to swallow my tongue. Was damn sure Drake had already slam-dunked his. Still, he managed a damn impressive poker face as Mrs. Perizkova stared expectantly at us—not a feat I could come close to touching—while Talia stammered to answer. Her eyes had widened with the force of a new expression, though whether it was embarrassment or frustration, I couldn't be sure.

"Mama!" she finally blurted. "I explained that to you how many times now?"

"Don't be sassy with me, young lady." It was clear where Talia had learned her ability for fierce glares. "You aren't too old to be taken over my knee."

My dick rose to full attention. Not one bit appropriate given the time, the place, or the company, but the thought of that perfectly shaped ass bent over for a few swats? *Jesus Christ*

Drake's cough shook me from my musings. The pained look on his face told me his imagination had just eased on down the same dirty road as mine. Luckily, Poker Face recovered more quickly. With a smooth-as-whiskey smile, he leaned forward. "It's a pleasure to meet you, ma'am. Your daughter is an amazing asset to the team at Stone Global, especially with all her new responsibilities. I was just speaking to the owner, Killian Stone, about a possible promotion."

Talia glared at Drake. Yeah, *glared*. Who the hell glared about a promotion?

Mrs. Perizkova provided the answer to that quickly

enough. "Hmmph. New responsibilities. She already works too much for a woman. It's no wonder she's first in line to become the next family spinster."

"*Mama!*"

"It's true, Natalia. And since these men are your bosses, someone needs to speak up for you, if you're not going to do it for yourself."

Talia put her face in her hands, physically shrinking once more. Watching the change in her was like getting wrapped in barbed wire. I refused to stand by and let it happen a second time, no matter how it affected the way her mother viewed me. I wasn't there for Perizkova brownie points.

Instinctively, I tightened a hand on Talia's shoulder until she raised her face for me. Only after ensuring her undivided focus did I finally speak.

"You are an amazing, talented, smart, and necessary part of our team. No one knows that better than Drake and I. Do not let *anyone* tell you otherwise. You single-handedly organized an entire product line launch. SGC would never be enjoying its exposure and success without you."

Before Tolly could voice a peep in response, I turned on her mother—the woman who should have been building her up, not tearing her down.

"Your daughter is in a league of her own among her peers, Mrs. Perizkova. If we were standing at SGC headquarters right now, I guarantee you I'd be backed by hundreds more voices. She has a promising future because of her insightfulness, awareness, and compassion. It would probably be best if you came to terms with that truth." When Tolly fidgeted beneath my hold, I clamped my grip tighter. "More importantly, this is what she wants. She has too much to contribute to the world to be sitting on the sidelines repopulating the earth. Not that I have anything against children"—I tossed a weary look around at the little princess mobs still running about—"but she is young and just hitting her professional stride. I can only imagine her abilities if she had a little family support."

Silence. Well, what could pass for it in this place.

Everyone, including Drake and Talia, just stared at me. Gawked? I couldn't—and wouldn't—debate the point. At the moment, for Talia's sake, I hoped I hadn't gone too far overboard and would be forgiven the outburst. I sure as hell wouldn't be taking it back. No way could I bear witness as her own mother whittled away her self-esteem. It hit way too close to home. I knew exactly what Talia was feeling inside. And I wouldn't wish that feeling on my worst enemy, let alone the woman I loved.

What. The. Fuck?

Had I...?

I hadn't.

Yeah. I had.

I'd just admitted it. Granted, to myself *thank fuck for small miracles*—but ohhh, yeah, I'd definitely gone there. And, I realized with a start, would happily do so again if need be.

I love her.

Yeah. I did.

"Is it time for cake now?"

Praise be for Anya.

Everyone in the crowd immediately started fussing, happy to have the diversion rather than deal with the diatribe I'd just laid out. I still wasn't a damn speck remorseful—until I turned toward Talia...and those huge brown eyes brimming with tears.

My stomach flipped over on itself.

Shit.

Sorry. I mouthed it, shrugging like a lame-ass.

She shook her head and dashed off, toward the little *princess's* room, I assumed. Though I longed to follow her, I was stopped by a gentle tug on my sleeve.

"Mr. Ford, a word?" It was Grandmother Perizkova, leading the way to some privacy in the corner. I had no choice but to follow—yet was relieved to see Drake heading toward the restroom. Probably to clean up my disaster.

The old woman's eyes narrowed, though her regard felt shockingly friendly. "You're quite a young man, Fletcher Ford. I can see why my granddaughter is so smitten with you." I must have looked shocked, so she went on. "Don't worry. She hasn't told us anything yet. I daresay she doesn't even know it herself." She grinned as though we shared a secret. "But a woman as old as me? I've seen it all, Mr. Ford. And the lot of you are in love."

Once more, my jaw fell. Still, I managed, "The...lot of us...?"

"Don't play coy. You know what I mean, Fletcher. And I'll bet you even know what I'm going to say about that, don't you?"

"Not in the least." *Not* a lie.

"I say..." She tugged me down toward her, making sure our gazes met. "Follow your heart. Clearly, she already has it in her hand."

And with that, she lifted her Cleopatra smile once again before turning on her heel and walking back to the party.

I could react with nothing but speechlessness for a few moments—before I, too, bolted into motion. On a determined pursuit of the two people who formed my component parts.

It was easy enough to find them. Drake and Talia were

huddled together near the back exit of the store. My steps slowed as I watched them. They were a magnificent sight, dark heads so similar in color, Tolly fitting so perfectly into the space beneath Drake's jaw. I almost turned around, not sure if she'd want to see *my* face after the hammer I'd just thrown into the party.

But then...her head jerked. I could damn near smell her awareness of me...sensing me near her, like she always seemed to...before she looked up. Her eyes glimmered. A warm, beautiful smile spread across her face.

I dared a few more steps closer. Had to clench back the rise of feeling as Drake swung his body out, opening their circle to include me.

A few more steps.

When I came within reaching distance, she wrapped her arms around my neck, pulling me in. It would've been rude not to hug her back, right? My arms felt so perfect around her tiny waist...so perfect. I pulled her tighter, all the way up against my body. Since my back was to the crowd, no one could see how intimate our embrace was.

"You're...not mad?" I didn't try to disguise the hopeful catch in my voice.

"No. Not even a little." Her smile turned tremulous. "Mama needed to hear that. *I* needed to hear..." She sniffled as she trailed off.

I tucked her in tighter. "*Tolly.* Why are you crying, baby?"

"It's just— I just—"

"What?" I brushed my lips along her hairline, yearning to do more. My whole body sure as hell begged for it too.

"I— I don't know how to say it all."

"Try," I urged. "Please. I don't ever want to hurt you

or embarrass you. Please tell us what's going on in there." I replaced my lips with a finger, tapping her lightly on the temple. She grabbed it, gathering up my whole hand and then lowering it over her heart. That did it for the corresponding part inside me. My ribs strained from the effort of keeping its thundering beats contained.

"It's what's going on inside here," she explained. "It's... in here." She patted my hand on her chest. "I'm scared. And overjoyed. And...so many things all at the same time. It scares me and confuses me."

Drake stepped in closer. If anyone was looking now, we definitely were not being discreet. I didn't think I cared anymore.

"Sweet, beautiful girl. Every single thing Fletch said over there was the truth, plain and simple. You need to believe it, and *they* need to believe it—and we're here to help."

She laughed softly. "Help, hmmm? Like locomotives plowing snow?"

Drake growled. "Maybe like trains...carrying passengers. We want to be with you while you grow, to help you believe how astounding and smart and dazzling you truly are. You need to surround yourself with people who will lift you up, baby—not hold you down. Do you get that? Do you see that was why Fletch got so worked up?"

"Yes." She sighed. "I do. And I *know*, but they're my family. It's not that they don't love me. It's *because* they love me. My mother and grandmother—they're old-fashioned. They were both brought up in another country, for heaven's sake. They have completely different ideals when it comes to how success is measured, and... What?"

Her self-interruption came on the heels of my snicker.

"Well"—the conversation I'd just had with Grandmother P replayed itself—"you might be surprised, Tolly—at least when it comes to one of those things."

"What do you mean?"

"Well...your grandmother just gave me a little *talkin' to*."

Her eyes bugged. "She did *what*? Why?"

I shrugged, even pressing the charm button a bit. "She thinks you're in love with us...*and* that we could make you happy."

Drake joined my soft laughter.

Talia jumped back as if burned. "No. She. Did. Not."

"Yes. She. Just. Did."

"Damn," Drake murmured. "Grandma's a dialed-in little lady."

Talia shook her head, setting free a cloud of sparkles. "That doesn't make sense. Or maybe it does. We all think she's been acting a tad senile lately." She finished by waving a hand, though she flashed a watery smile, as if already knowing her attempt at levity would be rebuffed.

"Talia." Drake wiped the grin right off her face with his drill sergeant tone.

"I'm teasing. But I don't want to talk about this anymore... please." She clasped her hands, looking like a princess grown into a queen. "Why don't we go get a piece of cake?"

My gut growled. "What kind?"

Drake's jaw firmed. "Cake is fine—but you *know* we'll finish this later. After I have a nice piece of—"

"Don't you dare finish that sentence, Mr. Newland." Yep. The queen was ready to rumble. "There are children everywhere."

He arched a brow. "Like I could forget?"

Again, as if cued by a stage director, Anya twirled her way over to us. "Auntie Talia, aren't you going to have cake? It's a really big one, with pink and blue roses, and Aurora and Elsa, and rabbits and butterflies." She peered up at Drake and me too. "My mama said you two could have some, since you're Auntie's friends."

"I would love a piece—of cake." I slid Talia a sexy grin. "I *really* hope it's chocolate."

"How did you know?" Anya grinned and grabbed my hand—the one *not* occupied with stealing a fast feel of my woman's delectable ass. Later, I'd blame Drake for starting the feel-up-fest—which he had. "Well, part of it is," the little girl went on. "And the icing is fluffy, not that yucky kind. I made sure Mama got the right kind this time. Last year, at my circus party? The goat from the petting zoo ate the cake!"

Anya towed us back to the heart-shaped table where the dessert was being sliced. She talked nonstop until we reached the others, covering every subject from rude goats to her favorite crayon colors to an upcoming trip to visit the Magic Kingdom princesses in a few weeks. "Look!" she cried out at last. "I found them. They were over in the corner, hugging. Weren't you, Auntie?"

"Anya, that's enough." Katrina—Anya's mother and Talia's sister—finally stepped forward to curb her enthusiasm. "Let's serve the cake. Then we can open presents."

The little girls chorused their wild approval of present opening. Apparently, the love of gifts started young in the XX genetic camp.

Fifteen sugar comas and at least thirty presents later, Kat declared the party a success. Drake and I, through a silent but mutual pact, had blended our way farther into the background during the gift opening—and thanked ourselves for it. We'd been treated to the pleasure of watching our girl interact with her family and the children. She'd been, in a word, amazing. Over the course of an hour, she'd captivated me in at least a hundred new ways. Always patient with the young ones, loving and gentle with her elders, she was everything a true princess should be.

That made it all the harder to process the tense air between the woman and her mother. I hoped our presence hadn't made things harder on Talia, but none of the other guests seemed fazed by the scowling and mumbling, so it would stand to reason that it was the nature of their relationship. This was definitely something we would chat about tonight—but not until after Drake and I made her scream our names a few times.

Maybe more than a few.

Tapping once more into the telepathic line she seemingly had to my brain, Talia lifted her head. Circled until she found my gaze...and met it. God*damn*. Her sexy brown eyes sparkled with new desire, and her lips parted in the tiniest, most perfect *O*.

Yeah. The woman could sure as fuck read me from across the room. The last time I'd beheld that look on her face, it was just after I'd made her come hard. My face had been buried between her legs, my cock aching to replace it.

I pushed up from the wall, arching a brow at Drake. He nodded in support.

It was *so* time to collect our woman.

We waded into the thick of the party again, saying polite but hurried goodbyes. Already, my body sizzled from the electricity between us. Drake appeared to have a fever as well. No goddamn way was Tolly *not* coming home with us. The only struggle between Drake and me would be who drove and who got to entertain her in the back seat.

I leaned toward Drake. "I'm so glad you drove, control freak."

"Fuck off," he gritted. "I've let you drive my Range Rover. Even while I was in it, which is basically putting my life into your hands. And besides, you had her *last* time on the way home, dickhead."

"RPS, then?"

He rolled his eyes at my suggestion.

Just then, Talia joined us. "What's RPS?"

I chuckled. "Rock, paper, scissors."

"Oh, is *this* the way high-powered executives make decisions these days?"

"When the stakes are this high, it's the only fair way."

"I think I'm afraid to know what you're trying to settle right now."

In a coordinated response that only came from years of close friendship, Drake and I answered, "You should be."

This story continues in
No Simple Sacrifice: *Secrets of Stone Book Six!*

ALSO BY ANGEL PAYNE

Secrets of Stone Series:
No Prince Charming
No More Masquerade
No Perfect Princess
No Magic Moment
No Lucky Number
No Simple Sacrifice
No Broken Bond
No White Knight

Honor Bound:
Saved
Cuffed
Seduced
Wild
Wet
Hot
Mastered
Mastered
Conquered (Coming Soon)
Ruled (Coming Soon)

The Bolt Saga:
Bolt
Ignite (July 31, 2018)
Pulse (August 28, 2018)
Fuse (Coming Soon)
Surge (Coming Soon)
Light (Coming Soon)

Cimarron Series:
Into His Dark
Into His Command
Into Her Fantasies

Temptation Court:
Naughty Little Gift
Pretty Perfect Toy
Bold Beautiful Love

**For a full list of Angel's other titles,
visit her at AngelPayne.com**

ACKNOWLEDGMENTS

To all of YOU, my readers, who have found this series and support it so much—THANK YOU!

And last, but certainly not least, to the one and only, most ruthless editor on the planet—Melisande Scott. You are the icing to my cake!

ABOUT ANGEL PAYNE

USA Today bestselling romance author Angel Payne loves to focus on high-heat romance starring memorable alpha men and the women who love them. She has numerous book series to her credit, including the popular Honor Bound series, the Secrets of Stone series (with Victoria Blue), the Cimarron series, the Temptation Court series, the Suited for Sin series, and the Lords of Sin historicals, as well as several standalone titles.

Angel is a native Southern Californian, leading to her love of being in the outdoors, where she often reads and writes. She still lives in Southern California with her soul-mate husband and beautiful daughter, to whom she is a proud cosplay/culture con mom. Her passions also include whisky tasting, shoe shopping, and travel.

Visit her at AngelPayne.com

ABOUT VICTORIA BLUE

International bestselling author Victoria Blue lives in her own portion of the galaxy known as Southern California. There, she finds the love and life-sustaining power of one amazing sun, two unique and awe-inspiring planets, and four indifferent yet comforting moons. Life is fantastic and challenging and every day brings new adventures to be discovered. She looks forward to seeing what's next!

Visit her at VictoriaBlue.com